# THE PERFECT SPY

# THE PERFECT SPY

## A CLEAN ROMANTIC SUSPENSE

## AMY MARTINSEN

Copyright © 2021 by Amy Martinsen

Cover design by Tracy Anderson (TracyAndersonPhoto.com)

ISBN-978-1-7343148-5-4

Printed in the United States of America

❄ Created with Vellum

# 1

-----

John Leeman stands off to the side and doesn't move his lips. Not once. Everyone else is talking but him. Reading lips is part of my tradecraft, but I mentally shut it off when I'm at headquarters. Not today, though.

The call came when I was running, something I force myself to do to stay fit, even on a muggy day in August. It also allows me to eat ice cream at the end of a long day. I have a freezer full of rocky road.

I'm Kate Ross, a CIA operations officer. I have to answer my phone no matter what's going on. But I was at the point in my run when I felt like I was dying, so I was happy to stop and answer it.

It was the call, though, that no CIA officer ever wants to get.

"Kate, the FBI are here. They've been debriefing the asset. He's talking about a bomb."

What air remained in my lungs rushed out and the trees lining the running trail blurred. I bent over, my hands on my knees, hoping for extra oxygen. A bomb threat on top of everything else.

The caller was one of the collection management officers in my division. The poor guy was assigned the details of this debrief. I'm sure when he was making a list of questions for the asset, he didn't expect to hear the word "bomb." And there's nothing quite like debriefing an asset who has turned against the Agency.

Assets from the Middle East, like this man, rarely live long enough for exfiltration. When discovered as spies, these assets are tortured and killed by the insurgents they spied on. I know this all too well. So, to look a turned asset in the face and ask why—why did he give valuable intelligence and the identity of CIA officers to the enemy—is a rare and difficult assignment and is happening in my division at Langley. And now there's talk of a bomb.

"Let me guess, he's not giving us a location," I said.

"Affirmative. They're bringing Eva in and the FBI isn't too happy about it. I thought you'd want to know."

"I'm on my way."

"I'll bring you up to speed when you get here."

Eva Calvo, a former Arizona Border Patrol agent, is a part of my team and very good at finding out the truth. But she's new and may need some backing, which is why I immediately came in and am now standing outside the debriefing room in a tank top, yoga pants, and sweaty hair slicked up in a bun. All dress codes die at the mention of a bomb.

The tension in the office grabs at my stomach. Instead of cubicles filled with dark-suited officers hunched over computers, there are frightened-looking faces orbiting the debriefing room, lips repeating the same phrases of shock and disbelief.

All but one.

Leeman is still standing off to the side, dignified with dark eyes that appear to take in everything. But his lips remain still. I pinch mine together. Why is he here and what is he thinking?

I catch Eva's eye as she comes in from the hallway. Shoulders back and chin high, she walks directly to me.

"Thanks for coming. Are you ready for this?" I ask.

"I'm ready," she answers.

The door to the debriefing room opens and warm, stale air rolls over us. The Agency isn't trying to keep our former asset too comfortable.

FBI Agent Maxwell's large frame fills the doorway, then steps out. I've crossed paths with him a few times and it was never pleasant. It looks like today will be no different. His lips are a straight white line in his flushed face. Sweat rings hang like broken hammocks under his arms. His gaze, blank with failure, focuses when he notices Eva and me. For a second, I wish I was clean and in my usual dark skirt and white blouse, but I brush the thought aside.

Maxwell comes up to us, glaring at Eva. "Well, if it ain't Officer Kate Ross. I heard you were coming. And bringin' me some so-called help." Here we go.

"Yes, Agent Maxwell, it's good to see you, too."

I hold out my hand. It stays out until he reluctantly shakes it. I fight the urge to wipe my hand on my yoga pants. His bad day is about to get much worse, or better, however he looks at it. No need for personal insults, though.

"This is Officer Eva Calvo, one of our new operations officers."

Maxwell glares at Eva.

Eva's eyes remain fixed on his.

Does Maxwell know what he's up against with Eva? He shakes her outstretched hand, and she doesn't hesitate to wipe her palm on her pants.

I pull my lips in to keep from smiling. I've heard several lectures from Eva on how quickly germs spread.

"We're going to let Officer Calvo take your place in the debriefing room while you take a break."

"Look, Ross, I just need a little more time with this guy. And I don't need a break." His telltale vein pulses to life on his sweaty forehead.

"You've spent twelve hours with this guy and all you've got from him is 'Allah is Great.' It's time to let someone else try," I say. We don't have time for arguments.

Eva's eyes fix on his and I'll bet the cost of a townhouse in Georgetown she hasn't blinked once.

Maxwell shuffles his substantial girth a few inches closer to me. I take a shallow breath through my mouth, trying to breathe around his body odor and the onion rings he ate an hour ago.

"I've heard about your little group of mommas. You've gotta be out'a your mind if you think that crazy Arab is going to tell this middle-aged widow from San Luis where the bomb is, or if there even is one." Of course he refers to her as a widow, ignoring her twenty-plus years as a Border Patrol agent.

"I'll get him to talk." Eva folds her arms. His bulk dwarfs her petite frame, yet she stands ramrod straight.

Maxwell looks down, surprised, as if he thinks she can't speak.

"I've been doin' this for years. Whatever it's gonna take to crack this guy, you ain't got it." The pulsing vein on his forehead goes into double-time.

"I'll get him to talk," Eva repeats.

I clench my hand into fists. We've got to hurry. "Maxwell," I say, "you know as well as I do that our intel, which at this point is a good guess, indicates we could have an attack on US soil by four this afternoon. It's ten o'clock, we have instructions to let Officer Calvo spend some time with our former asset. And she needs to do it now."

Eva's brown eyes narrow. "Officer Ross is right. We're wasting precious time."

Maxwell's vein is deep red and has doubled in size.

He looks at Eva and laughs, then elaborately motions for her to walk toward the door of the debriefing room.

"You think you can get him to tell you the truth? Be my guest."

"I don't think I can, I know I can," Eva says.

As Eva walks past him, Maxwell grabs her arm, stopping her.

"Who do you want to go with you?"

Her dark brows come together in question.

"You're not going in there alone, are you?"

She gives him a full, stunning smile and then carefully removes his hand from her arm. "I'll be just fine." She opens the door to the debriefing room and walks in.

## 2

The door to the debriefing room shuts with a neat click, but not before I glimpse a man in Arab dress slumped over a small table. It won't take Eva long, maybe ten minutes. But when the clock ticks on a bomb threat, time ceases to be normal. I force my hands to unclench.

Maxwell doesn't leave to take his much-needed break but stands next to me, arms folded over his barrel chest, staring at the closed door. This doesn't help the tension.

Reading lips, I roam through conversations in the room. Some are asking about Eva, some questioning the intel on the time frame, and some are franticly rehearsing lists of compromised officers.

With surprising reserve and stone-like lips, Leeman moves closer to us. The rumors of his good looks are true— he *is* tall, dark, and handsome. He wears his black suit well and doesn't appear to be neglecting his workouts. He looks foreign, but not. Are the other rumors about him true? This I know: he and Maxwell in the same view is a painful contrast.

After about ten minutes, the place erupts. Officers are running everywhere, shouting orders.

Eva slips out of the debriefing room and comes to us.

"There *is* a bomb, and it's set to go off in Los Angeles in three hours," she says.

Relief shoots through me and I touch Eva's arm in gratitude.

Maxwell gapes at us.

"He gave us the exact location and a team in LA is being contacted," Eva continues. "When the insurgents found out he was a spy, they threatened to kill his family. He didn't trust the CIA to get his family out of the country. He gave the insurgents all the information he had." My stomach rolls at what this means for the Agency and this man's family. I need something to eat. I inhale through my mouth and blink away a few black spots in my vision.

"How did you?" Maxwell stammers.

"I have my ways," Eva answers. She and I turn to go.

Maxwell grabs her arm and turns her around. "No. You gotta tell me how you did that."

She yanks her arm out of his hold. "You grab my arm one more time and you'll find out," she says.

He lifts both hands up, palms facing us.

"I'm sorry, I'm sorry," he says. "I just wanna know what you did."

Eva exhales through her nose the way moms do when they're irritated.

"Have you ever had to get a teenager to rat-out a friend? To tell you who brought the booze to a party or where they *really* spent the evening?"

He gave us a slight headshake.

"Well, I have, so when I say I have my ways, trust me, okay? And you can watch the tape."

He nods as if he doesn't know what else to do with his head.

"And you may want to brush up on your micro expressions. You have a vein on your forehead that practically dances when you're anxious."

I bite the inside of my lip, knowing she'd see this and say something.

Maxwell's right hand goes to his forehead. Then he quickly folds his arms but immediately drops them as soon as they touch his sweaty underarm fabric. The muscles in his jaw tighten.

"Now, you have a bomb to disarm and I have a three-cheese queso in the slow cooker and book club at seven, sharp. So, if you'll excuse me." She gives him the urging smile of a mother trying to make her point clear, then turns to me, ready to leave. A middle-aged mom has bested him.

"We know where the bomb is and have time to get to it before it goes off," I say before we go, trying to bring the big picture back into focus.

Maxwell just stands there, expressionless, as frantic officers swarm around him.

Eva and I walk past Leeman on our way out. I catch a subtle whiff of nice-smelling cologne and admit to myself it's a pleasant relief from the smell of onion rings and sweat.

**3**

---

The humidity is suffocating and I'm sticky with sweat after walking from my black Tahoe to my front door. I unlock it and walk into darkness. I used to always leave a light on before I went to Afghanistan and before my mother died. But not now. My keys and phone clink on the glass table just inside my door and I wince. The sound is louder in the dark. I flip light switches on as I make my way to the kitchen.

No one is here to greet me—I live alone. It's a single-level, two-bedroom two-bath house in Kensington, Maryland, giving me a reasonable commute to headquarters. My mother lived with me for a short while, when her health was declining. I have a small backyard with a cherry tree that she sat under to watch it bloom for the last time in her life. I took some time off work to recover from Afghanistan and to be with her toward the end. It was nice to have another heart beating within these walls, even if that heart was fading.

After seven years in the CIA and two assignments in the Middle East—one as a case officer—coming home to dark emptiness shouldn't bother me. Spies do most of what they do alone. It bothers me on days like today, though.

They found the bomb in a parking garage in downtown Los Angeles and quickly disarmed it. There had been barely enough time to evacuate the garage and two adjacent office buildings. Most of the people in the area went home from work knowing nothing about the dangerous threat that could have changed or even cost them their lives. These people knew nothing about the trained professionals that masterfully gained the information and eliminated this threat in order to keep them safe.

This is my job—to spy and lie and pretend and sometimes risk my life to find the truth. And no one knows about it.

I wish our former asset would have trusted us. The CIA has an exfiltration plan ready for any asset when they or their family feels threatened. Within hours we can have them safe and on their way to a new life. Even though this former asset thought he was doing the right thing by trading valuable intel to protect his love ones, the insurgents killed his family anyway.

Once I'm in the kitchen, I head to the freezer for what my run and this awful day earned me. I roll my eyes. Who am I kidding? If it were a normal day in December and I had skipped my run, I'd be doing the same thing.

I grab a pint of rocky road ice cream, pull off the lid, and throw it away. There won't be any leftovers. I grab a clean spoon from the dishwasher and head to my secret room. It's not hidden behind a wall panel in the basement, though that would fit a certain Hollywood profile. It's simply my spare bedroom.

I have no family who might come stay to see our nation's

capital over the holidays, or anytime. I have no friends who may come visit for a weekend. It's just me and an extra bedroom to hide my crazy.

I turn on the light in the short hallway and enter the doorway on the left. The hallway light casts strange shadows on the walls. For a few seconds I stand in the semidarkness. The rocky road has softened enough for me to scoop out a spoonful. The cold chocolate-marshmallow sweetness melts down my throat and my shoulders relax a little.

I flip the light switch on and admire weeks of obsessive work displayed all over the walls—charts, graphs, pages of notes with string connecting them to other pages of notes. And the occasional photo representing a victorious find— faces I have imbedded deep in my mind.

Nahla had been my asset in Afghanistan for over two years. I met her in the market, one of the few places women in that area could go outside their homes. I was pretending to be a relative of a local family, not a CIA officer trying to recruit assets. Nahla and I became market-day friends.

A few months after we met, a neighboring tribe massacred her village, killing everyone including her husband, six-month-old son, and extended family. Wounded and believed to be dead, Nahla's attackers buried her in a shallow grave with the rest of the deceased villagers. Somehow, she dug herself out and crawled to the nearest road. I was driving back to the CIA Compound when I found her. She was a wreck, physically and emotionally.

Since Nahla was a little girl, she had secretly longed to be free. When I told her she could have this freedom, and I could teach her how to fight for it, she didn't believe me. How could a woman have so much power? I'll never forget the smile on her face when I explained that if her attackers

believed her to be dead, she had a powerful secret weapon—
she could be invisible.

Nahla became one of the most valuable assets the CIA
had in the region, serving up several high-ranking terrorists,
leading us to weapon stashes, and giving us the locations of
many IEDs. Her beautiful name meant "a drink of water" in
Arabic, and the information she gave us was like a drink of
cool water in the hot Afghani desert.

Then someone told the insurgents Nahla was a spy, and
she died. I want the people who gave her up. That's what this
secret room is about.

The spoon comes to my mouth a few more times while
my eyes roam the walls, moving from one face to another. No
one knows about this room because I've been told explicitly
by headquarters not to find who gave Nahla up.

"There are officers in the field doing this." "You're
compromised and it's too dangerous." "Emotionally, you
need to heal." I know all the reasons I shouldn't have a room
that looks like *A Beautiful Mind* meets *Conspiracy Theory*. But
I don't care as long as I find these monsters. My eyes roam
from photo to scribbled notes to charts as I put a few more
bites in my mouth.

A scraping sound forces my gaze down. That's weird. The
ice cream is almost gone, and I barely tasted it. I spoon
together the last bite and eat it as I walk back into the
kitchen. I throw the container away and toss the spoon in the
sink. There are a few questions on the wall that will probably keep me up most of the night.

## 4

I'm paying for my night in the crazy room. I rest my forehead in my hands and close my eyes. My mind won't let me drift off, though. Not after the email I just read. When I open my eyes, I have a tunnel-view of my dusty computer keyboard and the large cookie crumb stuck between the V and B keys.

I take some canned air out of my side desk cupboard and blow the dust off. I catch the large crumb and quickly throw it away. The moms I work with have educated me on the impressive number of germs living on that crumb.

This lunch mess I can easily fix. It will take a much larger effort to fix what is waiting for me on my computer screen.

I read the email one more time. It's protocol, but I had hoped it would be someone else. I have a few minutes before my meeting with my boss, so I give Gina a call. I need a dose of her encouragement.

She answers the phone after just one ring.

"Hey, Kate." Her southern accent hums in my ear.

"Hi. I've got some news. You have a minute?"

"Of course. I'm gonna put you on speaker. Denise is here. I'm helping her with some profiling software."

"Hi, Kate," Denise says.

Calm and grounding, I'm grateful Denise is there. It would be nice to hear Eva's voice, too, but I'll talk with her soon. Since I've been home, I've been able to help train these women. They not only form a solid team, but are *my* friends—I'm not alone. Just the sound of their voices is settling.

"I received an email this morning. We have our first assignment."

It's been nine months since I lost Nahla and was immediately pulled out of the Afghanistan—persona non grata in a matter of minutes. Over these nine months, I have worked closely with Gina, Denise, and Eva, but this will be our first assignment together with me as the officer-in-charge. This team is a part of the "think outside the box" approach in the fight against terrorism—three middle-aged moms using their mom skills to catch the bad guys.

The cheering on the other end of the line brings a brief smile to my face. The excitement fades, though, as they register my silence.

"But because this is my first time in charge, I'm required to have another more experienced officer shadow me. It'll be Officer John Leeman."

"I thought no one wants to work with us." Denise asked.

She's right. It's no secret that the only reason they've given me this team is because no one with any operational experience would take it. It's also my boss's way of offering me redemption after what happened nine months ago.

I shake off this thought and sit up straight. The CIA Directorate of Operations and those on up believe they have found an untapped source in these women and I believe it too, which is why I named the team U-Tap.

"It's protocol. I guess Leeman drew the short end of the stick."

"Ya don't seem too excited to work with him," Gina asks. "Is there a reason?"

"No. Not at all. We're all professional. I guess I just don't like someone questioning my every move." I'm lying and I know they know it, especially Denise. She can spot a liar a mile away.

"Uh huh," Denise says, sounding unconvinced.

"Hey y'all, we'll make the best of it. And we have our first assignment as U-Tap. It's what we've all been working for."

Gina's enthusiasm is the lift I need. The subject of Leeman isn't over, that's for sure. These moms let nothing slide. But now is not the time. They've delivered the quick boost of encouragement I need before my meeting.

"We will. And it feels great to have our first assignment. I've got to go meet with the boss, but I'll let you know when the briefing is. And I'll give Eva a call and let her know the good news."

"We can't wait," Gina says.

"Whatever this assignment is, we can do it," Denise adds. Warmth expands my ribs and I exhale. My lips turn up at my computer screen. No matter who shadows me, I want to run U-Tap and see it succeed.

"Thanks ladies. You're the best. I'll be in touch," and end the call.

At a glance, Denise Reed, Gina Stoddard, and Eva Calvo appear to be normal looking middle-aged women—nothing out of the ordinary. In a crowd, they'd become invisible. Masterfully trained by the CIA, each possesses remarkable skills and knowledge. Now that terrorists are using mothers and children to wage their holy war, we need people who understand this world. And there's no one better than a mom who has been doing the mom thing for years. They make the perfect spies.

I read through the email one more time and close it. These women have proven they can do hard things. That's why the CIA worked so hard to recruit them. Can *I* still do hard things? Am I the right person to lead them? I standup, straighten my black skirt and jacket, and push my chair into my desk. Time to go meet with the boss.

The warm desert breeze dried the tears on her cheeks and rustled the branches of the mesquite trees surrounding her.

It would frighten most to be in the desert alone in the middle of the night, especially in the dangerous Arizona border town of San Luis. But Eva Calvo wasn't frightened. What could frighten her now, having stood at this very spot on a similar night and watched her husband and fellow Border Patrol Agent, die? He bled out despite their team's best efforts to stop the effects of a gunshot to his neck—a signature cartel kill shot aimed just above his bulletproof vest.

Eva looked down at her hands, still feeling the stickiness of trying to keep blood, and life, in her husband.

With the tip of her boot, she pushed dirt around and instinctively looked for his blood, but knowing in the same second it was ridiculously too long ago. The natural world and life's continuous march forward had erased this crime and her loss.

Is that why she felt compelled to keep a cross here, so it would force the world to remember her sacrifice?

Eva smiled as she knelt down and straightened the new cross she had just placed. She lightly touched one of the red silk roses. For those who saw the cross, it would be nothing more than a bright spot in the brown desert marking some-one's death. But for Eva it was personal—a reminder of her handsome husband handing her a bouquet of the long-stem beauties.

He would surprise Eva as she leaned over a hot stove, their children beaming the smile of security that comes from parents who loved each other. But later, after the children were in bed, he would take a rose and gently draw the tips of the petals across Eva's lips, followed by the touch of his own.

Eva stood and wiped the tears from her cheeks. There were too many now for the warm breeze to dry. She lifted her long, dark hair to cool the back of her neck and turned her head to face the wall. Glimpses of it were visible in the moonlight.

Living so close to the border, Eva had seen the eyes of those desperate to flee a corrupt society, and hardened eyes trying to bring their form of corruption to America. These two very different groups had motivated her to become a Border Patrol agent, where she met her husband. She worked alongside him for over two decades.

Eva retired, though, after that awful night in the desert. But she couldn't sit back in her grief and do nothing, so she had tried to effect change—actual change that could hope-fully bring a voice of reason and order to a broken system. She read everything she could on immigration reform and was preparing to run for city council when the CIA contacted her—they wanted her to bring her knowledge and experience, and loss, to the table.

Could she do it? At fifty? Was she strong enough?

Eva looked down at the red silk roses, then kissed the gold cross she wore around her neck and prayed for courage. She knew what she had to do and would need all the help she could get.

enise Reed knew this day would come. Her young
sons flew through the door of their apartment
and ran straight to the bedroom they shared.
Normally they found her before they took off their backpacks, talking over each other about their day at school. She
looked forward to this time of day, kissing each boy on the
top of his head and taking in the smell of the playground
and classroom and lunch she had packed for them. But now
they sat on their bedroom floor with scared eyes and tight
lips.

Gangs ran the streets and constantly needed new recruits
—frightened boys who could be brainwashed. Recruits
rarely made it past the age of sixteen. They were shot during
some drug deal or robbery gone bad.

Now her precious sons had been threatened directly.

The gangs never thought much about these losses,
they just focused on keeping frightened, silent boys
moving up in their system in order to take some dead
gang member's place. Gangs are a sick business that

protect turfs and dole out revenge in order to keep the money coming in.

Denise was a black single mother who was forced financially to live in a low-income, gang-controlled area in the Bronx. As a result, she fought a battle against helplessness. Sometimes she won, and sometimes she lost. But as she looked into the scared, silent faces of her sons, she vowed this would be a battle she would win.

Determined but not stupid, Denise knew she couldn't physically fight the gangs. So, she needed to outsmart them. She had always loved learning, ranking top of her class through high school. Every time she showed her report card to her grandpa, he'd smile and say, "Knowledge is power, baby girl. Knowledge is power." And she believed him.

College had always been a dream for Denise. But she was the oldest in her family and despite the scholarships she was awarded, the only way her family could survive was for her to work. She was fortunate to finish high school.

So, Denise educated herself through the public library and the internet. And she took her sons on this journey, showing them a larger world than the run-down city block they lived on. Just like her grandpa, she taught them that knowledge was power.

Denise immersed herself in the psychology of gang warfare, learning what strategies she could adapt to her circumstances. She was slim and of average height—a profile that could be easily added to in order to look different and forgettable. With a few alterations to her appearance and clothes, she could conceal her true identity while blending into a crowd—she could become invisible, one of the strongest advantages in battle.

Denise hated feeling invisible, though, particularly

around wealthy customers who frequented the upscale restaurant where she worked. It had bothered her so much she had considered quitting. The job paid well, though, and the more invisible she was, the more tips she earned. And she desperately needed the money if she was going to get her sons in better schools and eventually college.

But now something that made her feel powerless—being invisible—could become her strength. Disguised, she could study the gangs in her area and learn how they operated— what drove them and what scared them. She connected names with faces, the buildings they worked out of, and the cars they drove, all while appearing as just another black mom on the street that nobody remembers ever seeing.

Her hours of surveillance paid off. Denise taught her sons what to say and not say, and what emotions to display to convince the gangs that recruiting them would be more trouble than it was worth. She felt empowered and began teaching other mothers what she had learned. She also had the highest respect of the local police officers. After a while, the gangs began looking in other neighborhoods for recruits.

When Denise's sons eventually graduated from college, they gave their mother something she never thought she would have—a college degree.

Denise relished every minute in college, studying what she had a gift for—reading people. She earned an undergraduate degree in psychology and then earned a graduate degree in criminal justice, specializing in profiling. Her master's thesis outlined an effective way to fight inner-city crime, including her clandestine experiment. It impressed her committee chair, who worked for the Agency.

The CIA made Denise an offer.

It was an answer to countless prayers. At fifty-two, what

kind of employment could Denise find? Never did she imagine a job with the government. The challenge excited her.

But it would require some major changes. One of the most difficult would be the small circle of people who could know about it. As a CIA operations officer, Denise could only trust a few people with the burden of this secret. Her sons, of course, would be among these few. But even then, there would be much she couldn't tell them. Honesty and clear communication were one of the greatest strengths between her and her sons. Could she feel comfortable keeping so much from them? And was it fair to worry them?

Denise did what she had always done—she discussed this job offer with her sons. Through hugs and praise and tears of gratitude, it was clear what Denise should do. With the rock-solid support of her sons, she accepted the job.

Through eighteen years of marriage and three children, Gina Stoddard and her husband had experienced some challenges, but nothing like this. They had always talked through problems together. That was the biggest red flag—her husband quit talking to her.

A pornography addiction was something Gina never suspected, at least not in the beginning. Her husband hid it well because it just wasn't what a Christian husband and father did.

But when the addiction became too big to hide, Gina had to face the truth. Even then, she never thought her husband would choose pornography over her and their three daughters. After all, she'd been the homecoming queen. And she'd kept herself up.

But he did.

Gina had lived in somewhat of a bubble up to this point, not understanding how evil the world could be. Both she and her husband grew up in the small Georgia town they both still lived in. They had filled their lives with church, family and the tight-knit community of fellow Christians ... not pornography.

In high school, Gina excelled at computer science. She single-handedly transformed the yearbook from a dingy black-and-white relic to a colorful tribute to modern graphics. With the help of her guidance counselor, she applied for and won a two-year scholarship to the local junior college. She completed a year and then quit when she married.

As a young wife and mother, church service provided Gina with another outlet for her computer skills. The weekly bulletins and service flyers never looked so good. Once their daughters were in school, she worked a few days a week at the town print shop, ironically digitizing wedding invitations —all while her own marriage secretly crumbled one click at a time.

Now that the bubble had popped and Gina understood clearly the evil of pornography, she had to protect her children and others.

Not one to sit and stare at the wall, Gina had sought help from her preacher and a professional counselor who guided her toward a new life. Yet she couldn't get a handle on the constant frustration and lingering sense of powerlessness. She just wasn't having it.

Gina began looking for online programs that could safeguard young people from exposure to this illicit world but found most of them wanting. Frustrated, she signed up for some computer classes to learn more about cyber protection and breezed through them. Her mind spoke the advanced language of computer coding.

School gave Gina a much-needed outlet through those hard first years as a single parent. It wasn't long before she had a degree. For her capstone project, she put a software program on the market she was confident could not be hacked.

That's when the CIA came knocking at her door. Apparently, they were always on the lookout for such skills and found her ideas fresh and innovative. Though she could make much more money in the market of software design, she leaped at the chance to work with the CIA.

Her husband had chosen his life and now, at forty-eight, Gina was choosing hers. She was ready to catch some bad guys.

A s I round the corner to my boss's office, I smooth back the braid that holds my thick, black hair. Of my parents, my father, Ammar Rasheed, left the biggest mark on me, giving me his dark, Middle-Eastern features. They've come in handy on several assignments, especially in Iraq and Afghanistan.

He didn't give me his name, though. Ross, a shortened American version, was the name he gave my mom and me. It was also the name he used on every legal document except my birth certificate. Maybe this was his way of reminding me where he came from. Like I'm not reminded every time I look in the mirror.

Before my father left, he set up a trust fund that comfortably took care of us. He paid our house and car off, along with a life insurance policy for my mother. All this, yet no divorce. When my mother died, I used the money from the sale of our home in Huntington Terrace, Maryland, to pay off her medical bills. Everything I have now, I earned. What's left of Ammar Rasheed's trust fund remains untouched.

My father left when I was two months old. There are no pictures and my mother never talked about him, despite my incessant questions. Without my mom's input, our neighbors made up their own answers to satisfy why who they knew as Ammar Ross would leave his young family. It didn't take long before I heard the one theory that sent my life down the path I'm on now. Playing at a friend's house, I overheard her mom talking on the phone, explaining to another woman in the neighborhood that my father was a terrorist who went back to his people. She used the words "violent," "evil," and "horrible," all words I understood. But terrorist?

I ran the three blocks home, falling a few times and cutting my knee because the tears blurred the sidewalk. I tugged at the large *Webster's Dictionary* until it fell from the bookshelf. Kneeling on the floor, I opened it where it landed. Tears and snot and blood smudged pages as I turned clumps of them to get to the T's.

What was this word, terrorist? After sounding it out a few times, I finally found the right spelling. Vomit burned my throat, and I braced my arms against my stomach. Does my dad hurt other people in his country? Is he violent? I rolled off my heels and sat on the floor. Was this true? He left us. He left me, so it must be true.

That was when I quit asking my mom questions. I didn't want to know anything about my father. I would be nothing like him. I would devote my life to truth and peace and freedom. Imagine my delight when I discovered a government agency devoted to my quest.

I'm thirty-one now and with a master's degree in Arab Studies and access to the best people-finding resources in the world: I can find my father, but I don't want to. He has no place in my life. The only possession linked to him, besides his money, was my mother's wedding ring. She never took it off. A wide gold band, it would clink against a drinking glass or when she moved a vase of flowers. I buried her with it on her finger.

My mother knew I'm a CIA Officer. I figured if she never talked about my father, she'll never talk about me. And I wanted her to know what I do—that I find the truth.

I pull at the side of my eye, a habit I constantly fought in the field. The one genetic gift my mother gave me was her large, pale-blue eyes. Everyone who knew my mother tells me I have her eyes. It's the one thing that makes me happy when I look in the mirror—to see a part of her amid the dark features of a man I never knew and don't trust.

But even though they are my mother's eyes, I had to change their color to make me a convincing and forgettable Middle Eastern woman. Sand was constantly finding its way under the contact lenses I wore to turn my eyes a deep shade of brown. Though in many areas in the Middle East women have light eyes, I couldn't take the risk of being remembered and wore the contacts. Being a spy is all about being the person no one remembers seeing.

Neal Holt is chief of the Middle East division and my boss. His closely cropped gray hair never grows and his white shirt and dark dress pants never wrinkle. This outer military-grade stiffness is in direct contrast to his inner self.

Neal Holt is the closest thing to a father I've ever known.

Not only has he been my training mentor and field chief, but he and his wife of thirty-two years, Nadine, have made me a part of their family. They have three daughters and I am their fourth. Neal Holt was a pall bearer at my mother's funeral and Nadine held my hand through the entire service.

His office door is open—an unspoken invitation to come

in and have a seat. I step through the threshold and am greeted by his fit, smiling self, sitting behind his desk. And to his right sits John Leeman.

**9**

---

I keep my gaze forward, not wanting to look to my left and see Leeman. I need another second before I face him.

I've read his bio. He's thirty-three. His Japanese grandmother explains his dark features and exotic eyes. He wouldn't have to wear contact lenses in the Middle East. He's strikingly handsome and wears the same cologne he wore in the debriefing yesterday.

But I don't trust him. I've heard things that make me think of men like my father, things that make me question his character.

And when you put your life in the hands of the officer next to you, character is everything.

"Kate, I'm glad you're here," Neal says as he and Leeman stand up.

Neal's gaze scans to include both Leeman and me. Neal Holt always acknowledges those around him, no matter what. He knows all the janitors in our section of headquarters, the names of their spouses and children. It's the proper way to treat people and he expects it of those he works with.

I smile and politely nod, keeping my gaze forward two beats too long.

My boss's left eye narrows slightly. After over two decades in the CIA's clandestine service, including many assignments in the Middle East, the man has no tells. Neal Holt shows nothing unless he wants you to see it. And he wants me to see his left eye narrow. He knows I have a problem with Leeman and this arrangement.

I turn to Leeman and offer another polite smile and nod.

Leeman gives me a dazzling smile in return.

My first thought is that he could use that smile in the field, especially if he's managing a female asset. And that he probably uses it plenty in his personal life.

*That's not fair,* says the voice in my head. I swallow, then clench my jaw to hide it. This voice used to always be right. But now I don't know, especially when I'm around men I don't trust. I learned this the hard way nine months ago.

Neil and Leeman wait for me to sit in the chair to my right before they return to theirs. I angle myself toward both men because I already have a "private word" coming with my boss and don't want to make it worse.

"I'm so glad to have you both here," Neal says. "And I'm glad to have you on board with this idea of mine."

I looked down at my hands and grin. U-Tap is the brain child of Nadine, his wife, and me. But Neal had backed it and pushed it through to the operational level. By claiming the idea, he's putting his neck on the line. If U-Tap is successful, he'll give me the credit. If it fails, he'll take the hit. My career won't survive another failure. He is not only protecting me, but giving me a second chance. Maybe someday I'll tell Leeman this.

"As you both know, it's time we look at the fight against terrorism differently," Neal continues. "Jihadists are using mothers and children to fight their holy war. They're settling into our neighborhoods and our culture with patience we Americans aren't accustomed to. We need officers who understand this world. We need mothers and I believe we've put together a team of incredible women."

"I agree," I say in unison with Leeman.

He and I look at each other and then he chuckles and gives me another dazzling smile.

I do nothing but turn back to my boss and am met with his squinting left eye.

I look back at Leeman and bark out a forced laugh that's too late.

"If I may," Leeman interjects. "To be involved with U-Tap is an honor. I feel I have much to learn from you and your team, Officer Ross."

His voice is both sincere and sure—he isn't trying too hard. I didn't expect this.

I look back at Neal who is reading my every emotion like a book, a large-print, dog-eared, fall flat-open book.

I swallow and hold his gaze.

He squints his left eye.

"Kate, with this first opportunity to be in charge of your team, I believe John will be a great support. You both are well aware that U-Tap differs from anything the CIA has sanctioned before. It's uncharted territory and will require cooperation and flexibility, especially with law enforcement agencies." I mentally wince as Agent Maxwell's sweaty face flashes across my mind.

Leeman and I nod.

"Great. We'll have the briefing in a few days. That will give everyone some time to get up to speed," Neal says.

He stands, signaling the end of our meeting.

Leeman and I both stand and shake Neal's hand. I turn to leave but hear the words from my boss I know are coming.

"Kate, can I have a word, please?"

## 10

---

Cold sweat blooms across my face. *You're going to have to answer some questions,* says the voice in my head.

Leeman looks at me and our eyes hold for a second, a second I instantly regret. He's a skilled CIA operations officer, trained to read people. And in this one second, I have shown my vulnerability—an emotion I'm trained to hide.

I wonder the same thing I have been wondering for the last nine months—have I lost my ability to do this job? Did my instincts die with Nahla?

Leeman steps out of the office and quietly shuts the door.

Neal motions for me to sit back down and then pulls a chair over and sits facing me. He gives me the look that bridges all our past conversations—about work and trust and my parents. It's the look that brings us to the present moment. Rarely does Neal Holt beat around the bush. Never with me.

"What's going on, Kate?"

"I'm worried how Leeman will fit in with U-Tap." Not the complete truth, but it starts the words coming.

"What else?"

"I've heard things about him that have caused me to question his character. I need to know I can trust him," I say.

"What things?"

I'm not getting out of this office until I say it. I take a deep breath.

"I know he's divorced and has a little girl. I heard he abandoned her. His daughter. That he doesn't care about her." My eyes burn and I blink twice to cool them.

"Do you think it's true?"

*You don't know because you base this judgement on hallway gossip,* says the voice in my head. But what if it *is* true? What if he's just like my father? How could we work with him?

As an operations officer, I have to process massive amounts of intelligence and quickly determine the truth. I need to know, many times within a matter of minutes, if an asset is telling me the truth. I decide from the information in front of me and the voice in my head. They both have to work together because lives depend on it. But nothing's been right since I got back from Afghanistan, especially the voice.

"I don't know," I answer.

In the field, I have trusted Neal Holt with my life— meeting an asset, running surveillance, trying to gather actionable intelligence while pretending to be someone I'm not. This is the level of trust I'm used to. This is the trust I feel with U-Tap. And this is the trust I need in John Leeman.

"Katie, how are you really?" he asks.

My eyes burn again. I don't mind crying in front of Neal. I've cried in front of him plenty of times, but in the Holt's home on their sofa with the comforting presence of Nadine next to me. Not here. I don't want my co-workers to see me walk out of this office with red eyes. I will the tears back.

"Not so good," I confess.

"How's counseling going?" he asks.

I roll my eyes and then look at the floor. "Come on, Neal. You know how it's going," I answer.

Losing an asset and my mother within months of each other has won me several sessions of in-house counseling. But Neal knows I've quit going.

"You need to talk about it," he says.

I don't want to talk about it. I don't want to put words to what it feels like to lose two courageous women—one a brave asset and the other my mother. I want to let this unnamed pain pound around inside me and do whatever damage it feels I deserve. To give the pain words takes its power away.

*Listen to* . . . the voice says, but I cut it off.

"What about Leeman?" I ask.

"You can trust John. He's an excellent operations officer with a lot of counterterrorism experience, which is why I picked him to work with U-Tap. He's a man of faith. I see him and his daughter and mother at church each week. He has the same values you were raised with. And from what I've seen, he's a good father." I look down, my chin dipping to my chest. My mother had unwavering faith in God and taught me honesty, kindness, and moral purity—values I still practice despite my lack of Sunday worship.

"So why the rumors? Why have I heard the opposite?" I blurt out loudly.

"I don't know the source of these rumors, but I have an idea. I just can't confirm it yet."

I want to ask him what he's heard about these rumors,

but Neal says nothing about a person until he knows it's true. It's one of the many reasons he's trusted by the CIA and everyone he knows.

"Spend some time with John. Get to know him. Just because a man's marriage fails, doesn't mean he's like your father. And remember the core of what we do here."

I smile, knowing what his next words will be—not the unofficial CIA motto, that knowing the truth will set me free, but close.

"By their fruits ye shall know them."

He's referring to the bible verse in Matthew. The works, or fruits, of a person's life will prove their character. It's what Neal Holt teaches all who work with him how to judge and trust in times of uncertainty. It's my guide when all else fails, even that voice in my head.

I will need to see some fruits of John Leeman's life.

And I need to talk to Eva.

## 11

I give myself enough time to drive through Starbucks on my way to the Ronald Reagan Washington National Airport. I called Eva yesterday after my visit with Neal and told her about U-Tap's first assignment and working with Leeman. The office got her on an early flight, so I get us both a Trenta Dark Roast with two shots of espresso. She'll need it, especially with what I'm going to tell her.

When the Agency hired Denise and Gina, they both relocated to Maryland. Denise's two sons are married and living in other states. There's nothing keeping her in New York. Gina and her daughters, though still in school, needed a fresh start and were eager to leave the small Georgia town that knows all their business.

Eva has ties in San Luis. Her two sons and daughter are married and live there, as well as a large extended family. But more than anything, San Luis is where her husband is buried. She doesn't want to live anywhere else. When she's here, she stays with either Denise or Gina. Denise has a townhouse in Silver Spring that looks more like a yoga studio than a home. And Gina has a house in Wheaton-Glenmont that's overly decorated like a trendy boutique.

I haven't offered to have Eva stay with me and no one has questioned it. How could I with my crazy room?

So, Eva commutes and we are all fine with that. Sometimes it's necessary to charter a flight for her. Working for the CIA has its perks. But sometimes, like today, she flies commercial.

Eva reminds me of my mother—she takes nothing off of anyone, but is extremely compassionate. When I can, I pick Eva up from the airport so I can have a one-on-one conversation with her. And today we need to talk and not just about John Leeman.

Eva's waiting by the curb when I pull up, her black duffle bag over one shoulder and her arms folded. She's ready to get to work.

When she opens the back door to my Tahoe to put her duffle bag in, the humid air cartwheels across me and I sigh. When will fall come?

"How was your flight?" I ask. She gets in the front passenger seat and my chest tightens. Like my mother, she smells of fresh laundry.

"Good. I got some reading done." She picks up the coffee and takes several swallows. "Extra espresso. Thanks."

Eva always has a book with her and reads more than anyone I know. "What are you reading now?" I ask.

She ignores my question. "I want to know who John Leeman is and why you don't want to work with him."

Did I really think she'd let me avoid this? I grin at her and take a long breath through my nose. As I merge into freeway traffic, I explain what I've heard about Leeman and why it concerns me.

"But you don't know if any of these rumors are true. Do you have any facts? Anything to prove he can't be trusted?"

Eva always seeks the facts first. It's a quality that makes her an outstanding officer, especially when it comes to digging out the truth. But to analyze a situation takes imagination beyond the facts—to recognize motivation, context, and what may happen next. Eva needs to work on this.

"Just the voice in my head, which seems to get messed up sometimes."

"It gets messed up when you think someone, especially a man, is remotely like your father."

Is this why Eva reminds me of my mother? Because, like my mother would, she gets to the core of the issue in a matter of seconds? I'm sure Eva's kids didn't get away with anything, ever. Neither did I.

"You're right. And Neal thinks the rumors about Leeman abandoning his daughter are being spread intentionally," I say.

"Well, it wouldn't be the first time someone did that in this world. And it won't be the last." We both raise our eyebrows at this universal truth. But I still need to know for myself what kind of character John Leeman has. I need to see some fruits of his life, as Neal said.

"Neal picked him to work with us and shadow you. Let's get to know him a bit, then we'll have some facts to go along with the voice in your head," Eva says. She's smiling, excited to get to work. No unfounded rumors about Leeman are going to dampen her spirits.

I try to match her enthusiasm, but the next thing I tell her will dramatically change the mood in the car. As poor timing as it is, she deserves to know this before the meeting with the team in an hour.

"There's something else I need to tell you. Not about Leeman, but about our assignment."

"Yeah?" She motions with her hand for me to continue.

"We'll be working with the US Marshal's Office to transport a prisoner. It's Lupe Garza." Her head snaps toward me.

"He's the head of the Garza Cartel," I add.

"I know who he is," she whispers. She continues to look at me and I know her eyes aren't blinking.

## 12

L upe Garza grew up in a small town in central Mexico where the drug cartels were the controlling force behind everything. Fear of the cartels was a way of life—it was in the air everyone breathed.

Lupe lived with this fear until he had a growth spurt in the sixth grade. Within a matter of months, he was bigger and taller than anyone in his school. When a first grader kept Lupe from scoring a goal in a soccer game, he angrily shoved the small child to the ground. Lupe saw fear in the eyes of the child—the same fear everyone had in their eyes, except this time it wasn't the cartel's enforcers causing it. It was Lupe.

A switch flipped in Lupe's mind that day on the playground. He discovered his size and strength gave him a power over others, especially those smaller than himself. As time went on, that became everyone.

By the time he was sixteen, his gang ruled the streets of his town. By the time he was twenty-five, he ran a vicious cartel that was steadily killing or taking over the competition

until it eventually became the current-day Garza Cartel—
one of the largest and most powerful in South America.

A diverse bunch, the Garza Cartel deal in drugs,
weapons, gambling, extortion, rackets and prostitution.
They are responsible for a large percentage of drugs on the
US streets and a staggering number of deaths. Lupe runs his
cartel with a brutal efficiency that makes organized crime
from South America to Russia hot with envy.

At first, his brutality shocked his family, especially his
mother. His family hated the cartels, but they also enjoyed
the extra food and comforts Lupe's earnings brought them.
Poverty and hunger can wear people down. His family
slowly turned their heads and pretended they didn't know
what Lupe was up to. Today, they are one of the wealthiest
families in South America.

Lupe's rise to power was no hard-won discovery by intelligence and law enforcement agencies. He told his story to
everyone he encountered. His circle of employees and even
the local media outlets all listened, stroking his ego out of
fear. He believed himself to be the stuff that legends are
made of while those around him endured his obnoxious
tales so they could live.

With Lupe Garza, as with most narcissistic terrorists, his
ego tripped him up. Convinced he was invincible, Lupe got
sloppy and one of his "mules" was caught during a drug
smuggling operation. This mule was young and frightened
for his wife and children. He talked, providing law enforcement the intelligence to catch and incarcerate Lupe. It was
an enormous victory.

The mule didn't survive twenty-four hours in the Witness
Protection Program before one of Lupe's enforcers got to him
and slit his throat. His wife and children were brutalized and

killed on the same day, sending a message to anyone in the Garza Cartel thinking about talking for protection.

Tragically, the incident that provided Lupe's mule and eventually Lupe himself, happened on a dark night in the desert outside of San Luis, Arizona, just a stone's throw from the border. A brave US Border Patrol agent was shot and killed, Agent Mateo Calvo, Eva's husband.

With Lupe behind bars, most would believe the Garza Cartel crippled. But Lupe's power was vast and far-reaching, easily penetrating prison walls—even the specially crafted Supermax area at the Charles County Penitentiary. For Lupe, all this was an inconvenient and uncomfortable change of venue. He had the pesky task of running his cartel from his single-cell confinement, which he does successfully. The last four years have been extremely successful for Lupe. Business is booming for the Garza Cartel.

There have been two failed attempts to move Lupe to a different facility hoping to cut off his connections to his cartel. These have been costly failures, with the deaths of federal agents, law enforcement officers and civilians.

There has been chatter Lupe's men will try to free him during this next transfer attempt. As powerful as the Garza Cartel has become while Lupe was behind bars, no one wants to think of what would happen with Lupe physically back in charge. Whatever the cartel is planning in order to free Lupe, it will amount to more lives lost.

The government is desperate for a successful transfer and willing to try something new. That's where U-Tap comes in. But I need to trust John Leeman. And I need Eva to be on board.

## 13

Morning traffic in DC is awful, and we inch our way along in silence. Eva needs to process what I've just told her. Where Gina would start typing on her computer while thinking out loud and Denise would analyze everyone's emotions, Eva puts facts into logical sequence and place. She would understand my crazy room, though Deep-Dive-Gina should be the one I show it to. Denise would tell me what I already know, that I'm crossing the line. For now, I'll keep my crazy room to myself.

"I'll be okay with this," Eva says. I bob my head, hoping she'll keep talking. "I'd be lying if I said I didn't want to kill Lupe Garza and everyone connected to what happened to Mateo. But I won't." Her smile is more like a grimace, but it's enough to settle my mind.

Though an operations officer would rarely use a firearm, all three women have met the Agency's required qualifications on the Glock semi-automatic pistol and M4 rifle. Denise had a Concealed Weapon Permit and handgun prior to her CIA training. Eva, of course, had decades of weapon training as a Border Patrol agent. Gina, though, who had never been in a room with a gun, let alone fire one, turned out to be the best shot of the three.

"It will be okay if you help from the sidelines," I say. I feel her unblinking stare on me as I pull up to the security gate at headquarters.

We both show the guard our IDs and he waves us through. Her stare remains on me. I hope I'm never debriefed by her. "Okay, no sideline stuff," I say.

Her head turns forward, and she's smiling when I glance at her.

"Sometimes God answers prayers in unlikely ways. I've been praying for some closure with what happened to Mateo. Perhaps this is how I'll find it." I tug at the collar of my white blouse. She's prayed several years for this closure. When was the last time I prayed . . . for anything?

I pull into a parking space and turn off the engine. I shift in my seat so I can look Eva full on. Her shoulders are lowered and her breathing is even.

"Is there anything that will make this assignment easier for you?" I ask. I want to give her whatever consideration I can.

"It would be good if I drive. I don't think I'm a good enough shot to kill someone and drive at the same time."

I want to laugh, but I don't. "Yeah, you are. But you can drive."

We get out of the Tahoe and head toward the main entrance of headquarters and U-Tap's first meeting with Leeman. The warm air is heavy and thick with moisture and perspiration glues my blouse to my back.

Denise and Gina are waiting for us in the conference room. With her close-cropped hair, high cheekbones, and large hoop ear rings, Denise should be on the cover of a magazine. It's hard to imagine her blending into the streets of New York. Gina is about the same height as Eva, but with some soft roundness. She blames it on her mother's biscuits and gravy. Her blonde, curly hair is forced into a high ponytail and, as usual, she has a little too much makeup on. Denise, the tallest and the oldest, pulls the other three to her like a mother hen.

"Gina told me about Mateo and the Garzas. Are you sure about seeing Lupe, being close to him?" Denise asks Eva.

"I want to do this. Closure can come in strange packages," Eva answers. Denise purses her lips and nods.

"We'll all be there with you. You're not alone," Denise says.

"And let me tell y'all, I've got the info on Lupe Garza," Gina says. If Gina did one of her deep dives, she has more information on Lupe than any government agency.

The muscles gripping my neck all morning release and my shoulders drop. I'm taken in by the concern these women have for each other.

"Everyone's here. That's great," Neal says. I'm snapped back by the sound of my boss's voice and the subtle smell of cologne. John Leeman stands in front of me, hand extended, an appealing image of contrasts—his black suit with his white dress shirt, and his black hair with his gleaming white smile. I'm waiting for my "bad men can come in beautiful packages, so beware" training to kick in, but it doesn't. And this irritates me.

His grip is warm and strong. I awkwardly put my hand back to my side.

"May I call you Kate?" John asks. My eyes move to his at the sound of his voice saying my name. His dark eyes are a comfortable place to look, and this irritates me even more.

"Of course," I answer too quickly.

"Please call me John." I bob my head in agreement. My eyes stay on his and I want to reach up and slap them out of my head. What is John seeing in them?

"John, let me introduce you to these remarkable women," Neal says, saving me from myself. Neal had already greeted Eva, Denise, and Gina, asking about their families by name and remembering details about their lives. I would love to quiz Neal about John's life—especially about his daughter—but Neal is leaving that to me.

I watch as each of my team meets John. They smile, shake his hand, and exchange pleasantries. John seems impressed by the compliments Neal shares about each woman. The normalness of it untethers the voice in my head. *Maybe he's not such a bad guy.*

We each take a seat around the oblong conference table and I notice that, like Neal, John waits for us to sit down first. I wonder if John is queuing off Neal or if he has as good of manners as Neal. Few men do.

Neal hands out files and we dig into the details of moving Lupe Garza to his new "home." For the next several hours we discuss timing, vehicles, surveillance, tech support, and practice runs. As we go through the details and plans, Eva appears less tense and more engaged, and I'm relieved. I expect John to throw his weight around as my "shadow," but to my surprise, he contributes very little, allowing me to take the lead. Is this how he'll be in the field?

I'm hyper-aware of him throughout the meeting and try to ignore his shiny good looks that keep sliding into my peripheral vision. I want to leave as soon as it ends but am waylaid with questions—first some tech guys, then Neal, then Eva who's staying with Gina, wanting me and Denise to come over and eat enchiladas. I need to get out of here. I've shown this guy enough emotion for one day. Sweat beads on my upper lip and I shift my weight from one hip to the other. All the while, I see John standing by the door as if he's waiting for someone.

Finally, the last question is answered and the last person leaves and it's just John and me. I head toward the door like I'm holding a battering ram and almost make it through.

"Hey, Kate. Can I ask you something?"

## 14

"Can we meet someplace for a drink? I think we need to talk about some things before we work together," John says. This surprises me and I miss a mental step. Embarrassment flushes through me. Great. Did Neal tell him to do this?

"I don't drink," I say, because it's the first thing that comes to my mind. It's not just a put off. I really don't drink. Heaven knows I have plenty of reasons to turn to alcohol, but I won't give up my control, especially to something that tastes so awful. I'll drown my sorrows in rocky road.

"I'm not much of a drinker either. We can meet wherever you like."

"Have you been to Manny's Restaurant?" Thankfully, my brain's coming back in step. Manny's is usually quiet this late in the afternoon and has a great frozen lemonade. And I need a place where I feel safe.

"Yeah. I've eaten there a few times. Can I meet you there in an hour?"

"Sounds good," I say with all the professionalism I can

muster, which isn't much right now. Why does he bother me
so much? I grip my files like a security blanket and bolt out
the door.

MANNY'S IS a small Italian restaurant run by Manny Russo.
He took it over when his parents passed. The Russos were
Italian immigrants who brought with them some of the best
recipes Italy offered. My mother used to take me to Manny's
for spaghetti and meatballs, and it's the best I've ever had.

John is waiting for me out front. He's without his jacket
and tie, and the top button of his dress shirt is unbuttoned.
He's fresh and untouched from the oppressive humidity. I
had to park a block away and every sweltering footstep has
taken its toll. I'm wilted. The four round tables on the sidewalk are empty and somehow void of even the slightest hint
of invitation—more casualties of the heat.

John and I greet each other with a simple hi as he opens
the door for me. The familiar bell on the door jingles as cool
air filled with the smell of oregano and baking bread washes
over me. If I wasn't so anxious about why John wants to talk
to me, coming here would be a soothing way to remember
my mom. Instead, I've spent the last hour in an emotional
spin cycle, moving from humiliation to frustration to curiosity. But I will not let John see any of that.

Manny is large, loud, and always wearing an apron
spotted in red sauce and flour. This long, narrow room has
always been a safe place for me—my mother and I ate off
these same tables. It's all unchanged, even the menus
covered in the same grimy plastic. What Manny lacks in
upkeep, though, he makes up for in food.

"Katie Ross, is that you?" comes a booming voice from the back-kitchen window. Manny's large, floury body comes flying through the swinging door, expertly maneuvering his way through tables and chairs, coming within an inch of sending a chair sliding across the floor.

Out of the corner of my eye, I see John smiling as he looks back and forth between the oncoming Manny and me. Before I can get a word out, I'm enveloped by large, sweaty arms. "My Katie, how are you? The flower tree was blooming the last time I saw you, and why is that?"

Manny's has a cherry tree in front and each spring when it blooms, it's picturesque—a time when the four tables out front are in high demand. When I'd see the cherry trees bloom in our neighborhood, I begged my mom to take me to Manny's so we could eat spaghetti under the "flower tree." It's August now, and months since the cherry tree bloomed and months since I'd seen Manny.

"I don't know, but I'm not gonna let that happen again," I say. His meaty face breaks into a smile that brings with it a hundred childhood memories, the only difference is the sprinkle of gray in his full head of dark hair. He turns and looks at John and the smile drops from his face.

"Whatcha got here?" he asks, bobbing his head toward John. Manny is not only large and loud, but outspoken and very protective of me. My senior year of high school, my homecoming date brought me here for dinner. Manny took him in the back room for a "chat." When my date returned to the table, he was sweaty and his hands were shaking. He never asked me out again.

John smiles and holds his hand out. "John Leeman." Manny's eyes narrow.

"Yeah. I think I've seen you in here before." He turns

back to me as if John is an annoying interruption. "How are you holding up?" he asks, hopefully referring to my mom's death and not John's presence. Manny takes my left hand in both of his and lightly pats it.

"I'm okay. Busy at work." Manny, like most non-CIA people in my life, believes I have a job at the State Department that requires foreign assignments. It's best to keep your cover as close to the truth as possible.

"Well, don't let them work you too hard. What can I get you? You hungry? You look thin." I've been hearing these same words from Manny my whole life. If he had his way, I'd be his size. Between his pasta and my addiction to ice cream, it wouldn't be that hard.

"No, we'll just have a couple of frozen lemonades." Manny drops another smile as he looks at John with a "you're still here?" expression on his face.

"Okay," he answers with a sigh. "Sit wherever you like." He heads back to the kitchen slowly, shoulders slumped. I've seen this posture enough to know he's disappointed he can't stuff me to the brim. Nothing makes Manny happier than feeding people. But as much as I'd like to make him happy and stuff my face with whatever he has baking in the oven, I don't want to turn this into a dinner with John.

Booths line each wall of the narrow restaurant. Out of habit, I head toward the booth in the back, where my mother and I always sat. John waits for me to sit first, showing Neal-like manners but also allowing me to have the side of the booth with a full view of the entrance. For most, this would mean nothing more than giving me a choice of which side of the booth I want. But for spies, this is a grand gesture that doesn't go unnoticed—he's giving me the control to watch everyone who comes and leaves.

We slide into the booth except there's no sliding involved. The seats are covered with a dated cloth that forces you to lift your lower half a few inches at a time until you're where you want to be. I grab the table and perform this feat awkwardly while John does it in one fluid motion.

"So, it looks like you've known Manny for a while," John says. I try to adjust my pants leg that has twisted around my thigh, but my key fob in my pocket is in the way. I really need to lift my behind up one more time, but refuse to and try to ignore it.

"My entire life. My mom would bring me here when I was little." His dark eyes soften.

"I'm so sorry you lost your mom. Tell me what she was like." This isn't what people usually say when offering condolences—they tell me what *they* think she was like and then try to change the topic as quickly as possible. No one asks me what *I* think she was like. For the second time today, I don't know what to say.

"Here ya go. Two of the best frozen lemonades in DC." Manny sets two large frosted glasses in front of us, each filled with yellow slushy ice surrounding a large scoop of vanilla ice cream. Each glass has a cherry-red straw in it. He lays two cloth napkins with two spoons on the table. "You need anything, anything at all, I'll be right in the kitchen," he adds, facing me.

"These look great, Manny. Thank you," I say. John tells Manny thank you as well, but is completely ignored. Manny makes eye contact with me and thumps the table twice with one of his sausage-size fingers before walking away, a signal that if John does something I don't care for, Manny will take him in the back for a "chat."

I take a sip to keep from smiling. The mixture of

lemonade and melting ice cream is a rush of sweet, and I close my eyes for a second. I want to sit here alone, in silence, and let the lemonade lower my core temperature while taking me back to my childhood, but I can't. "I'm sure you didn't ask me here to talk about my mother," I say.

The bell on the door jingles and two women walk in. Both are in their early fifties, dressed for an upscale office job but no crazy heels, which means they're probably done competing for men. Divorced, most likely, because neither is wearing a wedding ring and obviously not rushing home to cook dinner. They're eating heavy Italian food, most likely with a couple of beers, at four-thirty in the afternoon because they can. I log this in between a blink. Operational awareness is hard to shut off sometimes. So is my ability to read lips.

John starts to look over his shoulder to see who walked in but catches himself. For the first time since I've met him, he looks uncomfortable and I smile to myself because my pants leg is cutting off my circulation. He takes a big swallow of lemonade and his eyes wince with what appears to be an instant brain freeze.

Manny slides through the tables and chairs like a lithe ice skater instead of a three-hundred-fifty-pound Italian man. He greets the two women, escorts them to a booth, and promises to return with water and menus. I have a clear visual of one woman's mouth and may catch enough of their conversation to prove my assumptions.

I smile and motion with my hand for John to keep talking. I left the conversation ball in his court before I cleared the front of the restaurant from terrorists.

"I need to talk to you about my daughter, Olivia." I'm going to take another sip, but stop and look up at him. For all the rumors I'd heard, I didn't know his daughter's name. "What have you heard about her?" I'm liking John's straight-forwardness.

Even though the two women are sitting on the other side of the restaurant, Manny makes a point to walk close to our table as he brings them water and menus. I ignore him.

"I've heard you're divorced, that you have a young daughter who you have turned the sole care of to her mother, your ex-wife. Supposedly you don't care for your daughter." John slowly shakes his head and closes his eyes. When he opens them, they appear to sag with pain—an expression I've learned is almost impossible to fake.

"I am divorced. I have been for two years. My ex-wife and I have joint custody of Livvy. When we divorced, I had a cottage built on my property for my mother, who knows I work for the CIA and what it demands. She's the only one I entrust Livvy with when I can't be there. I love my daughter and treasure every minute I have with her." My heartbeat slows and my lungs settle into an exhale. All my training tells me this man is speaking the truth. *He is,* says the voice in my head. Can I believe it?

"So why the rumors?" Manny walks closely past our table again, deftly balancing a platter with a basket of bread and two beers for the women. I catch the one woman say something about an ex-husband while her eyes narrow.

"I guess the best answer for that is we can't do what we do without some enemies. And when someone wants to hurt you, they go after the ones you love." I nod my head in agree-ment. "If I had heard what you heard and then had to work with that person, I would have questions. So, I wanted to talk to you. To tell you these rumors aren't true, that I love my daughter. I would do anything for her."

This last sentence comes out with a breathy desperation that makes me wonder if there's more than rumors he needs to protect his daughter from. At this point, I'm pretty sure that John Leeman loves his daughter and has supposedly gone to great lengths to provide stability for her.

"Did Neal tell you to talk to me about this, about these rumors?" The words are out of my mouth before I can stop them. John shakes his head and chuckles.

"I know what's being said about me. I don't need Neal to point out that people who may have to put their lives in my hands could have questions about my character. You're being asked to work with me. At the very least, I can give you and U-Tap the truth."

"Thank you," I say. I wouldn't have minded if Neal had orchestrated this meeting, but I'm glad it was all John's doing. It shows a little more of the "fruits" Neal spoke of. "I had concerns. We need to trust you, and if the rumors were true, it would be hard. You know as well as I do that in our line of work, we don't have the luxury of assuming the best in people. We have to know the truth." John holds my gaze for a few seconds, and I feel that same comfortable feeling I had before the meeting earlier.

"You're right. That's why I wanted to talk to you. So you would hear this from me."

My ice cream is melted and I take my spoon and swirl it through the lemony slush. "How old is Olivia?" I lick my spoon off and set it on the napkin. I'll just need the straw from here on out. John's eyes soften at this turn in the conversation.

"She's four. She'll be starting preschool in a few weeks." A cloud of worry seems to pass over his face. I imagine that first bit of letting go for a parent is hard. He looks at his watch and his eyes grow larger. "Speaking of which, she and I have a date tonight with a Paw Patrol movie." I smile, assuming that's the latest children's movie parents will soon grow to hate.

"You better not be late," I say with exaggerated concern. He laughs and raises his eyebrows.

"Never. Not for Paw Patrol."

I catch Manny's eye as he walks past our table with two heaping plates of lasagna. He delivers them to the women and comes directly to us. The one woman is describing her ex-husband's younger, thinner wife with slicing hand motions.

"We need to go, Manny." We maneuver out of the booths, much to the relief of my thigh. Blood rushes through it in a tingly wave. Manny gives John a side glance and then looks directly at me.

"It's on the house, Katie. You need to come back and let me feed you, though."

John pulls out his wallet and hands Manny a twenty-dollar bill, twice what the lemonades cost. "This is on me and I'll bring her back."

Manny's bushy eyebrows raise and gives John a quick nod. "You got yourself a deal." Manny turns to me and opens his big arms for a hug goodbye. He walks us to the door, telling John when would be the best nights to bring me back. That he's talking directly to John is a sign that John has passed a test. Manny will probably treat him well next time he comes.

I thank Manny again, and John and I walk out. I glance at the two women as I walk by, but both of their mouths are busy eating. I hope the lasagna and beer can take the edge off. The one woman should think about taking up an ice cream habit.

"Which way did you park?" John asks as he scans the street. I'm doing the same thing, noting who's around us and what cars are passing. It's a comfort zone he's probably eager to return to after sitting for an hour with his back to the door.

"I'm about a block this way," I say, pointing to my left. He walks in that direction, making the declaration that he's walking me to my car. "It's about a block down," I repeat. "You don't need to walk me." John smiles and keeps walking.

## 15

I t's cooled off a little, but not enough to lure people onto the sidewalks. There are two people across the street both talking on their cell phones. But on our side, we have a clear shot to my Tahoe. I'll never be comfortable talking where others can overhear me. I wonder if people understand how much information they give up talking on a cell phone in a crowd. Yet, it's easy to feel isolated with a phone in your hand.

"You never told me what your mother was like." After learning what I have about John and his daughter, I don't mind answering this question. But I take a few seconds to gather my thoughts. I'm sure he's read my file and knows the facts—that she was born Catherine Moore and raised in the Midwest. John slows his pace and looks ahead to my Tahoe.

"She was warm and approachable. If you were around her for any length of time, you would feel comfortable talking to her."

We stop at the side of my Tahoe and John turns and looks at me. His eyes are safe and I keep talking. "One of my earliest memories was standing in line with my mom at what I later learned was the DMV. All I understood was that everyone in that line was grumpy and didn't want to be there. By the time we got to the counter, people were smiling and laughing and it was because of my mom. That's who she was."

"I'm sorry the world lost her," he says. I swallow against my tightening throat. He's right. It's not just my loss, but a loss for all who could have known her. I move my eyes from his and try to assess my surroundings or read someone's lips, but nothing has changed. Why have I allowed this man to see so much? *Because he's safe,* says the voice in my head.

"Hey, I don't want to be the reason you're late for Paw Patrol."

He smiles but doesn't look at his watch. "I'll take the blame. Thanks for talking to me. We've got a lot of work to do in the next few weeks. Are you okay working with me?" I don't really have a choice, but that he's asking makes me grin.

"I'll see you bright and early tomorrow." He smiles all the way to his eyes, then turns and takes off at a jog for his car. *Is he safe?*

ALL EYES ARE on me as I walk into Denise's kitchen. The red splatters on the counters pop against the monochromatic setting. She, Gina, and Eva are cleaning up what looks like the remains of putting together a few pans of Eva's enchiladas. From the aroma coming from the oven, I'd guess they're about halfway baked.

"So, how'd it go?" Gina asks as if I'd just had my nails

done instead of meeting with a man we'll all need to trust with our lives. Denise and Eva watch me closely, analyzing my silence.

I lean up against the kitchen counter and take the glass of iced tea Denise hands me. "It went well. Better than well."

"Where'd' you go?" asks Eva as she continues to wipe smudges of enchilada sauce and bits of grated cheese off the counters.

"I had him meet me at Manny's." A slow chuckle rumbles through the kitchen. They've been to Manny's many times and know what he's like, especially when I show up with a stranger.

I sit down and share the meeting with them, sparing nothing. They're impressed by John's directness and the supposed care he gives his daughter. They also thought it was pretty amazing he gave the surveillance side of the booth to me. Their clandestine training taught them just how big a gesture that was.

Gina opens her laptop and begins typing. "It checks out that he requested building permits a couple of years ago for the home address we have on file at the Agency."

"What about the mother? Does she list the same address as his?" Eva asks.

"Yes. I have a Rose Leeman at the same address, starting not long after the city completed the final construction inspection. Also, John's divorce finalized when he said it was and granted joint custody." It always amazes me how quickly Gina can find out stuff about people.

"So those facts check out," Eva says, pulling a chair up next to me.

"Do you want to see a picture of them, the ex-wife and the daughter?" Gina asks. I swallow and then nod. I always find it sad to see a divorced couple together. In this case, they aren't actually together, but having just been with John, it feels like it.

Gina turns the laptop around as I scoot my chair closer to the table. The face that's starring back at me is fair, with blonde shoulder-length hair and blue eyes. Her smile seems to come from a happiness that can't be touched, especially by the sadness required to end a marriage. This is the part I don't like—a divorced couple was once so happy they celebrated with the commitment to spend the rest of their lives together. So, what happened?

"Her name is Clare. She works at Harrod and Raynott Financial, an international finance group. And here's a picture of Olivia." Gina turns the laptop to face her, clicks a few things and then turns it back for me to see. Olivia is a perfect blend of her parents—chocolate-brown hair that looks like John's hair diluted by the blonde of Clare's. Olivia has dark eyes with just enough of her oriental ancestry showing through to make them smiley. Her fair skin is her mother's and her smile is her father's. She's adorable, and John's declaration of love for her rings through my mind.

"How did you feel when John was telling you about Olivia?" Denise asks.

"I felt like he was telling the truth." I pause and take a swallow of tea. "There was that peace there, you know, when someone speaks truth. I could feel it." They all nod with understanding. The Agency has trained us to recognize truth, to know how it feels when spoken, as opposed to a lie. It's the foundation of intelligence gathering, and if you don't have an instinct for it, you're in the wrong line of work.

But have I lost my instinct? Can I trust what I felt with

John? I push the questions down with another swallow of tea.

"So, what he said checks out. Neal recommends him. I'd say we trust him out there in the field. Give him a chance with our support," Eva says.

"I agree," Denise says. "He had a good vibe about him."

"I agree with all that stuff. But y'all can't ignore the fact that the guy is totally hot. I mean, seriously, James Bond material. He should be on a recruiting poster for the CIA or something," Gina says. The room erupts into laughter as the timer on the oven goes off.

Gina's a huge James Bond fan, which largely contributed to her confusion, and dismay, that the CIA refers to their employees as officers, not agents. Foreign assets, who we recruit and spy for us, are referred to as agents. This tripped Gina up so much that Neal has us refer to foreign agents as assets.

We all grab pot holders and remove two pans of shredded beef enchiladas smothered in Eva's secret red sauce. We wrap up one pan for Gina to take home to her daughters and one remains with Denise, Eva, and me. We spend the next hour eating and joking about how we can recruit Manny to the CIA and turn him into an Italian spy.

## 16

W e're in what looks like a deserted warehouse at the outskirts of St. Charles—just one of the CIA's many "invisible" staging areas that we're using for Lupe Garza's transfer. There's a swamp cooler running, but it's nothing against the muggy morning air. It's been like this for the past two weeks, so it's no surprise I'm already sweating. It doesn't help that I'm dressed in dark leggings and a long-sleeved T-shirt—not exactly a cool summer outfit, but one of the many precautions for what we're about to do.

Our caravan consists of a gray older model minivan, a large weathered panel van with a local cable company's logo on the side, and a new dark gray Prius. Denise will drive the Prius, running a surveillance route once we hit city traffic. She's dressed in a dark skirt and light blouse—she's any DC woman heading to work. Denise has a good deal of practice blending into crowds and chose her own profile—nothing remarkable with her hair, makeup, or jewelry. Anyone who glances at her driving would forget her immediately.

The panel van will hold Gina and a tech team helping her run communication. For the last half hour Gina's been testing everyone's earpiece by cracking jokes and teasing John, who is also in all black. She's calling him a James Bond wannabe. It even makes Eva laugh. If you're teased by Gina, you're in. And it looks like John's in. Working with him the last two weeks has been easier than I thought. Like in our planning meeting, he lets me be in charge. And he's not afraid to get his hands dirty, running many practice runs scrunched in filthy service vehicles.

The gray minivan looks like any other not-so-new family vehicle that has seen its share of road trips and car pools. On the inside, though, it's a state-of-the-art machine that would make the real James Bond's and Q's mouths water. The tech guys really outdid themselves.

From the outside looking in, each window shows the normal seating configuration of a minivan with an open cargo space in the back. They construct these windows of a high-tech glass, much like a green screen used for visual effects in movies. From any angle looking in, one would see the expected family paraphernalia—a few toys, a soccer ball, some groceries. What they wouldn't see would be a bullet-proof shell loaded with cameras, recording devices, and two CIA officers armed with guns, tasers and tranquilizer guns. And no one will see one of the most notorious drug lords in the world heading to a new prison.

We have another fifteen minutes before we leave and I watch my team carefully. Each woman has had experience around really bad guys, but there's always the fear—of not enough protection, of something going wrong. I feel that fear even though I've been up close and personal with some of the worst human beings on the planet. The fear has to

work for you, to keep you focused and cautious. You can't let
it stop you. It's comforting to know that Neal is watching
everything live, and we have a large SWAT team ready at a
moment's notice.

I've had pep talks from Neal daily, but my early morning
call from Nadine this morning was a much-needed mental
boost. This is our brainchild, and she wants it to succeed as
much as I do.

"I've been praying for you, Katie, and your team.
Remember that when you're frightened," Nadine said. Guilt
curled in my stomach. Prayer was the one thing I hadn't
done to prepare for this assignment. I offered a quick mental
plea, but it rang hollow.

It was not for a lack of confidence that Nadine said
"when" not "if" I felt frightened. Fear is a part of all we do,
and she's been married to Neal long enough to understand
this.

My gaze moves from woman to woman, assessing where
they are with their own fear. Gina uses humor to deal with
stress. In some ways, I think this is one of the healthiest
coping skills to have. When it comes to getting the job done,
though, Gina is one hundred percent dependable. Denise is
centering, doing some breathing exercises. I've seen her do
this before and it makes her unflappable in the field. Eva is
serious and calculating, reviewing times and sequences,
allowing the facts of the mission to assure her. If she can stay
focused on driving, following the route, and hitting check-
points on time, it will help her handle being in the same
vehicle with Lupe Garza.

I feel John watching me the way I've been watching my
team. He's probably wondering how I'll handle this ride so
close to Lupe, not to mention the fear that our plan

somehow leaked out and there's a cartel ambush waiting for us. If it's going to happen, it will be on what we've been calling the long stretch—a five-mile section of both forested and open road that separates the Charles County Penitentiary and the outskirts of St. Charles. I've gone over every section of that road at least a hundred times in my mind and driven it with the team a dozen.

"It looks like your team was born to do this," John says.

"They've had plenty of practice at being invisible, whether or not they realize it. The stakes just haven't been this high before."

"You're right about their practice. But can there be any higher stakes than keeping your child safe? I think they've experienced these stakes thousands of times." John says, his gaze looking past me. With all the bad John has seen, he must be really overprotective of his daughter. "Do you think Eva is okay with this? With Garza in the same vehicle?"

"She says she is, so she is. I trust her completely. If she weren't up for this, she would say."

"How are you doing?" he asks. I swallow and smile at the same time—not very convincingly, I'm sure.

"I'm ready. You're gonna be wowed by some mom skills." There's a brief crackle in our earpieces and Gina's voice comes on.

"Ladies, it's time to rock-and-roll. Just a reminder that all comms will be on throughout this entire party and I'll be calling y'all by your names except for Officer Leeman. Unfortunately, there's a John in my tech van, so Officer Leeman will go by the code name 'Bondman.' We can't have things gettin' confusing now, can we?" Laughter erupts over our earpieces as John smiles and waves to Gina just as the doors to the panel van shut. He's taking her teasing well. I admire a man who can laugh at himself.

"John, I think you have a new name. Trust me, it could be worse," Denise says as she shuts the door of the Prius.

"You got that right. He's new. I had to take it easy on him. Can't scare him off," Gina replies.

"I'll be Agent Bondman as long as I get to work with you ladies," John says. We clued him in on Gina's officer-agent confusion and her disappointment of not being referred to as an agent.

"Smart answer," I say, and I hear muffled chuckles from everyone. He and I head to the minivan where Eva waits behind the wheel.

## 17

J ohn and I get in, each through a sliding side door. It feels awkward with everything open throughout the interior of the van—there's nothing to sit on but the floor and nothing to lean against but the door panel. Should something happen, all three of us need to get to Lupe without impediments, like seats or a console. I feel all arms and legs as I position myself and my equipment as comfortably as I can on the floor. The only thing lacking for John and me is a view of the horizon. I watch John and see how he does it, and he, too, seems to switch around to find the best position.

From the inside out, the van windows act as normal glass and I see the fake cable logo of Gina's tech van drive past, followed by Denise in the Prius. It will take us about thirty minutes to get to the prison. Along the long stretch are several side roads with forested coverage. Gina will position her van along those to stay within ten minutes of the mini-van, providing her with drone coverage of us. Once we have Lupe, Gina will never be more than a few minutes from us.

Denise will wait for us once we hit city traffic, to run a surveillance circle around us as we make our way to the US Marshals and an airplane that will take Lupe to his new home. For security reasons, none of us know Lupe's final destination, but if I had to put money on it, I'd bet his new home is at ADX Florence in Colorado. It's a Supermax where the worst of the worst go and where Lupe belongs. Our job is to deliver Lupe to the airplane by noon or sooner, depending upon traffic. Beyond that, it's up to the US Marshals.

"You two snug back there?" Eva asks as she fastens her seat belt. She looks like a middle-aged mom who just dropped her teenagers off at high school. She's wearing a plain gray T-shirt with jeans and tennis shoes. With her long dark hair in a ponytail, and no makeup or jewelry, she's unremarkable—the goal of every spy.

Both John and I give an okay and Eva starts the van. The air conditioning comes on full blast and John and I smile. "Who do I thank for this amazing AC?" I say. A few male voices chuckle in my ear.

"No thanks needed, but these tech guys are going to need a good lunch when we're done here, just sayin'," Gina says.

"I'll tell you what," Eva says, "we get this monster to where he belongs and lunch is on me." We all consent. It's one more thing that may help Eva through this. She loves to feed people.

For a few miles we ride in silence, except for the occasional exchange between Gina and one of the tech guys. The van takes a couple of turns and the buildings we've been passing become fewer and separated by patches of trees.

"We're heading into the long stretch," Eva says. John and I look at each other and nod.

On the inside of each door panel is a screen that, as John

and I sit across from each other, provides us with footage from cameras on the outside of all the vehicles as well as the drone. Gina controls what we see, giving us the best view possible. It still doesn't feel as good as sitting up in a seat and looking out the window. Maybe that's a spy thing, wanting to see firsthand what's going on.

On the screen next to John, I watch as Gina switches from the van-level view to the drone above and back. Everything looks as it should.

"I'm pulling into Starbucks right on schedule," Denise says.

"Copy that, Denise. Man, could I use a Starbucks-something-strong-and-creamy-with-sprinkles," Gina responds.

"Sounds good to me, as long as it's shaken, not stirred," John adds.

"Good one, Bondman," Gina says through everyone's muffled laughs.

Denise will drink her tea and scroll on her phone for a few minutes and then run a surveillance detection run to the next checkpoint.

"No one's following me," Denise adds.

"Copy that, Denise. Try to enjoy your tea," I say.

"I'll at least look like it on the outside." I know exactly what she means. To pretend to be someone else, you must be emotionally convincing even if you're so nervous you feel like throwing up.

The trees disappear and we enter an open area. If I were going to ambush us, this is where I would do it, though on the return trip with Lupe. I feel a nudge on my shoe and look up. John gives me a quick smile and mouths, "It's okay." I don't know what expression I had on my face, but it must have warranted some encouragement. I smile back and nod.

"How you doing, Eva?" John asks.

"Doin' great, Bondman. There's not a thing out here. I have a good feeling about this," Eva replied.

"Copy that. There's nothing but us out here. And everyone thinks Lupe is being switched tomorrow," Gina says. I give John another smile. I appreciate that the only times he's chosen to exert his authority, if you can even call it that, he does it by encouraging my team and giving me assurance. It's what Neal would do. I know Neal is watching the feed but letting me and John run this. It feels good to know he's out there, along with a large SWAT team.

We enter another patch of trees and I know when we come out of it, we'll have a visual of the prison. I watch on the screen as trees blur by, then glance at John. He looks extremely good in black.

I blink. Why would I think that right now? I squint at the trees, forcing my focus on them. From the corner of my eye I see John looking at me, but I won't look back—he'll see what I'm thinking. Gray prison walls flash across the window and I swallow.

## 18

I've seen Charles County Penitentiary many times in the past few weeks, and each time it reminds me of an ashen-gray factory from a Dickens novel. Today is no exception. The morning cloud cover and mugginess is holding on, giving everything an eerie cast.

"We have a visual of the prison," says Eva.

"Copy that," Gina replies. We drive in silence, John and I focusing on our screens as the prison and its razor-wire fences become larger.

"Approaching the first gate," Eva says.

"Copy that. I'm already in contact with the guards," Gina says. As the minivan comes to a stop, I brace my feet on the floor to steady myself. I don't want to set my weapon down for even a second. John does the same.

Eva goes through the rehearsed exchange with one guard while the other opens the front passenger door and runs facial recognition on all three of us. It's just a few seconds before we're given the green light to proceed. The huge gate opens and we drive forward.

"One down. One to go," Gina says.

"Copy that," Eva says. We drive a short distance and turn left around the first of three buildings. We drive to the end of the second building and stop for another gate. Another rehearsed exchange takes place between guards and Eva, another huge gate opens, and we drive forward. The third building is Lupe's Supermax area, and we stop in the middle of it by a door. Though it would have been easier and quicker to pick him up at the first building, we didn't want to give him or any of his "in-house" cartel connections the slightest sign of his early transfer by shuffling him to a different building. This far in a prison, though, and the gates will close in on you.

John and I open our doors and step out of the minivan. Eva remains behind the wheel but can see everything on a screen she has on her dash. She pushes the button that opens the back lift gate.

"We're out of the van and in position," I say.

"Copy that," Gina says.

"I'm leaving Starbucks and heading to my next checkpoint," Denise says. The sound of her voice calms me a little. Everyone is where they should be.

"Copy that. Right on time," Gina replies. John gives me a nod of assurance.

We wait by the prison door for a few minutes. Out of long habit, I scan my surroundings. The place appears deserted. There is one watchtower almost directly above us with two snipers at the ready. I look down to the first building and see another tower with two more snipers. The snipers are ours, pretending to do a practice run for tomorrow's transfer. We're being watched on a few cameras inside, though the prison is trying to be "business as usual" to not tip off anyone of Lupe's early transfer.

There are just a handful of people who know this is happening today. The big show will be tomorrow, which I'm sure everyone in the prison knows about despite Lupe's limited contact with prison personnel and next to no contact with other prisoners. Somewhere within these fences, though, are men working for the Garza cartel, being paid to convey information to Lupe so he can keep his "business" running. It feels good to have a hand in stopping it.

The door of the building opens and my heart leaps. Lupe fills the doorway and I immediately begin to breathe shallow —he stinks of meanness. I've smelled this kind of stink many times, especially among terrorists in Afghanistan. He is enormous, hairy, and covered with tattoos.

I feel for the syringe of Benadryl in my vest pocket. From prison records we know Benadryl causes Lupe to be extremely drowsy. For a drug lord, he's a weak sauce. John notices me touching my pocket and we exchange looks. All the encouragement he's offered me these past weeks runs through my mind and for the first time I admit to myself I'm grateful he's with us.

The guards have Lupe's hands cuffed from behind and leg irons clank with his every move. His blindfold has been duct taped into position at my request. We're brave but not stupid—we don't want Lupe Garza to see any part of us.

Two prison guards flank Lupe. They're large men yet appear small next to Lupe. One guard is pale with red hair and the other has brown hair. Both seem to be in their late twenties. They guide Lupe to the rear of the minivan.

"Whoever's driving, I hope you're ready to die today," Lupe bellows. His teeth are yellow and his breath rancid.

"No one's dying today," says the red headed guard.

"I'll second that," Gina says. "I like this guard. Get his name. I'll bake him somethin'." Only Gina could make me smile at this moment. Eva's shoulders twitch.

None of us will speak until Lupe's earplugs are duct taped into place over his ears. I don't want him to identify any of us. It's amazing how people can remember a voice.

The guard pulls Lupe's sleeve up a few inches. I quickly swipe his upper arm with an alcohol swab John has ready and inject Lupe with the Benadryl, a double dose for his body weight just to be safe.

Lupe screams a stream of expletives while the guards insert his earplugs and run duct tape around the circumference of his hairy head to hold them in place. The duct tape will be a bummer coming off, but it's a spy's best friend. The stuff has saved me many times in the field.

"Someone's got a potty-mouth," Gina says and I hear Denise chuckle.

The guards force Lupe into the back of the minivan, lay him down, and pull a black blanket over him. He's squirming like a cow that can't get up and he's changing the volume of his swearing like someone who can't hear themselves—a sign that his earplugs are working. We watch in silence until it's obvious the Benadryl is taking effect—his motions are slow and exaggerated, and he's slurring his obscenities. My heart rate slows down a little.

The guards nod to John and me, and the red headed one shuts the lift gate and checks to make sure it's secure. He runs his fingers across the school bumper sticker on the back window.

"I have to tell you officers, I think this is a genius idea," he says. The brown-haired guard bobs his head in agreement.

"I tell ya, I like this one," Gina says.

"Thanks. We think so, too," I say. "But let's not celebrate until sleeping beauty here is where he needs to be."

"Time to go," Gina says.

John and I thank the guards and get back in the minivan. I see Eva looking at Lupe on her screen and then her rearview mirror. "He's huge, and he stinks," she says.

"Copy that. You doing okay?" John asks.

"I'm fine. Grateful to be a little distance from him," she replies.

John and I look at each other and then at Lupe, an enormous snoring mound just a foot away from us. It's always a surreal feeling when the meet you've planned for months happens—to share the same space with the person you've spent countless hours studying. I've been in all kinds of odd situations in the field, especially in Afghanistan. But crouching in this minivan with John feels different, not because he's judging my performance—I don't think he is. It's like having to do a really grimy job, like cleaning a toilet, with a nice-looking man that smells good.

We drive back through each gate and guard station, Gina checking us through and Eva giving rehearsed phrases. As much as I disliked feeling trapped inside the layers of gates and fences of the prison, being out in the "open" with Lupe feels worse. I mentally run through the list of people who know we're moving him a day early. Did someone sell us out to the cartel? Lupe shifts and grunts, and I catch a whiff of his soured breath.

"I'm pulling out onto the long stretch," Eva says.

"Copy that. Everything looks clean as a whistle. I don't

see any traffic until you get to the highway," Gina says. We timed it that way—no visitors, no deliveries, just us. But if the cartel knows, they will try to free Lupe in the next few minutes. My eyes move from the screen to the windows to Lupe and back. John could look like Bozo the clown and I wouldn't notice now. He has the same focus on his face.

"I'm at my next checkpoint and beginning my surveillance run. You got this, ladies, and Bondman," Denise says.

"Copy that, Denise. And thanks," I answer.

Lupe shifts again and the blanket slides off his face. It's strange to see the innocence of sleep on someone so evil. The silver duct tape divides his face in half, smashing his hair against his cheeks in a childlike way. He was once his mother's darling two-year-old toddler, perhaps with long baby-like curls that would smash against his cheeks from his afternoon nap.

I jerk back and my heart explodes in my chest. The sound is so loud John and I lift our weapons and Eva swerves the minivan.

## 19

"Lord have mercy, was that what I think it was?" Gina asks. The smell is so powerful as it rolls over John and me, we instinctively cover our faces with our shoulders.

"If you mean was that Lupe, the notorious drug lord passing gas, then copy that," Eva answers. She gags a few times, the stench having made its way to the front of the van.

Round-eyed, John and I look at Lupe, then our screens, the windows and back at Lupe. My concentration is off and it appears John feels the same—he's looking everywhere. When we make eye contact, my eyes are watering from the smell.

"Well, they weren't kidding," Gina says. "According to Lupe's records, the prison has treated him several times for irritable bowel syndrome. Perhaps the stress of the day has caused his IBS to flare up." I can hear the background laughter of the tech guys.

"With my sons and their friends, I consider myself a professional in this area," Denise says.

"But when they told us we'd be using our mom skills to fight terrorism and organized crime, this particular skill didn't come to mind," Eva replies.

Lupe passes more gas and John and I push our backs against the van walls.

"What I wouldn't give to roll the windows down," John says. Bile burns the back of my throat. Of course, we can't take the chance of even cracking a window. I give him a look as we both cover our faces with our shoulders again.

"Now's probably not the time to tell you that Lupe's prison nickname is Gassy Garza," Gina says. I bite the inside of my lip to keep from laughing. The tech guys explode with laughter but are suddenly quiet when I'm sure Gina gave them one of her silencing looks to keep the comms clear. "We're halfway through the long stretch. Everything looks clear," she adds, back to business.

I've been counting the clearings and know exactly where we are without having to look at the screen. The distraction had loosened the knot in my stomach, but it's back now. We're almost at the prime ambush spot.

Lupe lets loose again, and this time it sounds nonhuman. It's so loud, it rouses Lupe from his Benadryl-induced nap. He swears in English, sleepy and slurred. Then he speaks in Spanish. I know enough Spanish to get by and can pick out some names of cities and towns. His voice becomes steady and commanding, as if he's giving instructions to someone. After a few more sentences, most of which I don't understand, I see Eva's head turn to look back and then snap back toward the road.

"Are you getting this?" Eva asks in a whisper. I look at John and he gives me a slow, spectacular smile. He's fluent in Spanish.

Lupe says a few more sentences and then pauses.

"We're getting every word and translating it as he speaks," Gina answers. "He's giving up names of cartel members, drug routes, all kinds of good stuff."

"Send everything he says up line as fast as you can," John says.

"Copy that."

We drive the rest of the long stretch on radio silence, the only sound being Lupe's side of a drug-induced conversation and the unpleasant results of his IBS issues, which we hardly notice considering the intelligence we are gathering. I wish I could understand all that he's saying, but the delighted look on John's face tells me we're getting a bonus to our plan.

"The main road is just ahead," Gina interjects during one of Lupe's pauses. Thirty seconds later, we merge into city traffic. Denise spots us and runs surveillance as we weave our planned route through freeways and suburban streets and back to freeways. The minivan, with its normal family clutter visible through the windows and its middle-aged driver, blends in with hundreds of other common-looking vehicles to become invisible . . . all while a gassy drug lord in the back gives up his secrets.

ALL THREE VEHICLES pull onto the small airstrip at the same time. We park by a JPATS plane, a part of the US Marshal's Justice Prisoner and Alien Transportation System, which is the largest transporter of prisoners in the United States. If you're getting a ride on a JPATS plane, your life, like Lupe's, is about to change for the worse. There's a line of US

Marshals that looks amazed to see us. They surround our minivan as soon as we stop.

John and I get out our side doors as the rear lift gate raises. Eva is at my side in three long strides, looking grateful to be out and breathing fresh air. Denise joins us and stares at Lupe, this being her first encounter with him. Three seconds pass before she turns her head and exhales.

One of the deputies reaches a hand out to me. "I'm Deputy US Marshal Thompson and we're thrilled to see you. I can't believe you pulled this off. To think you got Lupe Garza to us in a minivan!" He continues to shake my hand as he's talking. The other deputies are inspecting a groggy sounding Lupe along with the inside of the minivan. I can tell by their expressions and comments, they're impressed. The tech guys are standing off to the side, but it's apparent by their smiles they can hear Thompson's praise of their work. What the tech guys have in store for tomorrow's fake transfer would blow their minds. It's one thing to see spy "toys" on paper, another thing completely to see the toys in action.

Lupe appears to have registered the stop and swears in English. His words are clearer and he's making complete sentences, so I take out the extra syringe of Benadryl I have in my vest pocket. We administer the shot quickly and the deputies and John transfer Lupe to a back door of the plane and into the waiting arms of three deputies. I see their faces wince at the stench and I scrunch my nose. Have we briefed them on Lupe's IBS? Thompson pauses before he shuts the door.

"Officer Calvo, I understand this man and his cartel made you a widow," he says.

"You're right," Eva answers. Her eyes are shiny in the dull midday light.

"I think it's only right that you close this door." He steps aside and Eva walks up to the side of the plane. The sound of Lupe thrashing and swearing abruptly stops when Eva slams the door. She stands there for a few seconds and then walks back to us. I wrap my arm around her shoulder while Denise and Gina move closer.

"Thank you," Eva says to Thompson.

"No, it's us who should thank you, all of you. You've done a brave thing that's going to help stop the Garza Cartel. It won't be the last we hear of U-Tap." Warm pride fills my chest. "Like you already know, we can't tell you where we're taking Lupe, but we can let you know when he's safely at his new home in the Rockies," Thompson says with a wink. My guess about ADX Florence was right. "Thank you, again. And we're looking forward to tomorrow."

"Record Lupe during this flight. He gave us some great intel on the way here, among other things," Eva adds. I bite back a smile.

"Will do," Thompson answers and nods to us and then to the tech guys and John, who is standing next to them. Consistent with his leadership so far, John remains in the background allowing my team and me the credit.

Thompson walks to the front of the plane, is up the ladder in two steps, and closes the door. A few seconds later, the plane taxis to the runway and takes off.

We all head back to headquarters. Our celebrating goes as far as a much-deserved lunch for the tech guys, compliments of Eva. We all have a lot of paperwork to do and a phone call to wait for, though I'm sure it will be tonight before we get word from the deputies whether Lupe arrived at his new prison.

I try to focus on my reports but find all I can think about is whether the cartel is waiting for Lupe's plane to get in the air so they can shoot it down. My stomach twists in knots thinking of all that could happen if someone told the cartel connections in the prison of Lupe's early transfer. *They want him alive*, says the voice in my head. That makes sense. Shooting his plane out of the air comes with a small guarantee of Lupe surviving.

One by one, my team finishes their reports and leave, each with a hug from me. Eva looks satisfied but, like us all, would like to receive the phone call telling us of Lupe's safe arrival. We'll know before our meeting in the morning, where some real celebrating can happen.

I haven't seen John since we returned to headquarters, but I assume he has his own pile of paperwork. I finish mine and leave. There's no one here to tell me goodbye, and it feels odd after working so closely as a team today.

It's still light when I get home. I quickly change into yoga pants and a tank top and am on the running trail in a matter of minutes. The heat of the day has given way to a cool evening, which helps me not hate this so much. And there's the ice cream waiting for me.

I'm checking my phone constantly and have my ring volume on high. Most people would use some wireless headphones, but years of training has changed that for me—I will never put myself in a position where I can't hear what is going on around me, especially the footsteps of someone coming up from behind. If I ever wear any kind of headphones, they will be part of a disguise to trick others into believing I can't hear them.

The exertion of running is just as painful as always but necessary if I want what's waiting for me in my freezer. I do my usual four miles and arrive back home sweaty and exhausted. Still no call.

I lay on my living room floor in front of a fan and try to get my breathing back to normal. The cool air feels good and I close my eyes for a minute. Just as I'm sinking into that first level of sleep, where the surrounding sounds become nonsensical, my phone rings. My mind tries to convince me the sound is several other things before I register it as the call I've been waiting for. I look at the screen. It's John. I thought it would be Neal calling. I slide my finger across the glass and say my name as a greeting.

## 20

"**L**upe's there," are John's first words. I close my eyes and exhale. "You did it."

"*We* did it," I respond.

"No, you and your team did it. I just went along for the ride."

"I'm glad you were there," I say before I can even think. I *was* glad he was with us. "So, Lupe Garza is really in his new digs in Colorado?" John chuckles.

"Yep. Safe and sound. And there's been chatter that Garza's men are going to show up tomorrow. Man, I hope so."

"We'll be ready for them. I thought Neal was going to call everyone?"

"He is. And you'll probably be getting calls from some happy women pretty soon. But I asked Neal if I could call you first. I hope that's okay."

"Of course. Is there something you needed to talk to me about?"

"I wanted a chance to thank you for taking me on for this

assignment. It's not easy having someone watching over your shoulder."

"You're right. I wasn't too excited about it."

"Well, you didn't need me there. Whatever U-Tap's next assignment is, you're ready to lead." My throat tightens a little. These are words I've wanted to hear for a long time, but never more than in the last nine months. I always imagined them coming from Neal, though.

"Thank you," I say, my voice breaking a little. I hear some movement on John's end and a child's voice says "Daddy." My mind connects a voice to the picture of Olivia.

"Can you hang on for a second?" John asks.

"Of course." John does nothing to muffle their exchange and I hear his softened voice tenderly trying to coax his daughter back to bed. The best way to learn the character of an asset, or anyone, is to see them in dramatically different situations and study how they adjust.

It's not a stretch, though, for me to hear this softened version of John with Olivia and connect it to the John I rode with in the minivan today—because John cares. I saw how much he cares for his daughter when I was talking with him at Manny's and I saw how much he cared for my team's success today. *This is real*, the voice in my head says. I'm not eager to question these words like I was two weeks ago. I listen as more quiet exchange turns into a power struggle, with John losing. I grin as John tries to compromise.

"Who are you talking to?" Olivia asks.

"Her name is Miss Ross. I work with her," he answers.

"Miss Ross," Olivia repeats, and I wince at how stern it sounds. "Can I see her?" John exhales slowly, and it registers in my mind that he might give in and ask me to go on

FaceTime. I run my hand over my sweat-dried ponytail and dig my finger in the corners of my eyes for smudged mascara.

"Kate, would you like to meet Olivia?" he asks, defeat ringing clear in his voice. Olivia giggles in the background.

"I would love to."

"Thanks. We'll call you right back."

The return call was immediate, and the screen shows a distorted view of the little girl I'd seen on Gina's computer.

"Remember, hold the phone away from you so the other person can see your whole face. They don't want to see just your mouth or just your nose," John patiently instructs and Olivia giggles. It's a playful, trilling laugh that I instantly love. Did I ever laugh like that?

Olivia's face comes into focus and her smile is victorious. She has a missing lower tooth and half-dried hair, probably from her nighttime bath. John holds the phone out further and I see both of them from the chest up. Olivia is wearing a pajama top with a character from an animated movie on it and John's wearing a gray T-shirt. His hair is slightly wet but just-showered wet, not sweaty-wet like mine. I risk a glance of myself on the small screen in the corner of my phone and sigh. Why didn't I take a shower when I got home from running?

"Hi Olivia. I'm Miss Ross but my name is really Kate. Miss Ross sounds like a mean school teacher," and I make a face that brings back her wonderful laugh. I look at John and ask, "Is it okay if she calls me Kate?" realizing I just undid his attempt at enforcing respect for adults. He smiles and I see the same smile on his daughter's face.

"How about Miss Kate," John offers as a compromise.

"Miss Kate," Olivia repeats.

"That works for me," I say, grateful to have not undone John's parenting.

Olivia looks at me for a few seconds and then touches the screen with her finger. "You have pretty eyes, Miss Kate." Warmth blooms inside my chest. Never have I been happier to have my mom's eyes.

"Well, thank you."

"She *does* have beautiful eyes," John adds. He holds my gaze with his for a second and that comfortable feeling comes that I felt a few weeks ago in the conference room, except this time I don't want to slap my eyes out of my head. I want to keep them right where they are.

"Can Miss Kate read the book with us?"

"I bet she will if you ask her," John answers.

"Miss Kate, do you like *Goodnight Moon*?" Memories flood my mind.

"Oh, I love that book. My mother used to read it to me when I was little."

"I'm gonna go get it," she declares and disappears out of the screen. I hear bare feet slapping on a hard floor. John's face fills the screen.

"Thank you," he says.

"Of course. She's darling. This will be the best part of my day," I answer. His smile goes all the way to his eyes.

"It's always the best part of mine," he says.

"I have it," Olivia says amid foot slaps. John has moved to sit on a sofa of soft-looking brown leather and Olivia climbs on his lap.

"Should we turn the screen so Miss Kate can see the pictures, too?" John asks. I see Olivia bobbing her head.

"I want to do it," she says. Her finger slowly moves toward the screen, and then I'm looking at the green-and-red book cover. My shoulders sink a little at the image of the moon through the window.

John reads, his voice steady and soothing as he says goodnight to different items in the room. I see Olivia's finger point to each item as he says them, sometimes moving ahead of his reading. I smile as I remember memorizing my favorite storybooks and knowing when my mom would try to skip parts to speed up bedtime.

John passes the phone to Olivia and stands up, holding her. I see her cradling the book and glimpse her sleepy eyes. He's carrying her to her bedroom, passing through a living room and down a hall. All the while John is quietly saying goodnight to objects they are passing. I remain quiet, not wanting to rouse her.

The screen changes to a jumble of images and I hear the rustle of sheets as he lays her in bed. John whispers goodnight and I hear a kiss.

"Goodnight, Miss Kate with the pretty eyes," Olivia says. John's throaty chuckle blends with the rumple of moving blankets. The screen flips and his face appears. He winks as I hear a door pulling shut. We're silent until I see the brown leather of his sofa behind him.

"She's a beautiful little girl," I tell him. His expression is soft with love. "Why would someone want people to believe you don't love her?" I'm sorry I say this as soon as it comes out because his face hardens in an instant.

"I don't know. Neal and I are looking into a few things."

"I'm sorry I believed those rumors. It was unfair of me to do that. My dad left when I was a baby and, I don't know, I guess I'm pretty quick to judge." I rarely talk to anyone about my father, especially people I haven't known for very long. But after seeing what I just saw—not just how he treated his daughter, but how she responds to him—I needed John to understand why I misjudged him.

"I'm sorry someone is doing this to you. If it's any comfort, I can tell you love Olivia by how she responds to you, like she receives this kind of love every day."

"Thanks." For the second time since I've met John, I see his eyes sag with pain. "She does every time she's with me." The implication that perhaps there's someone who doesn't give her this kind of love hangs in the air. Could his ex-wife possibly mistreat this beautiful child?

"Hey, I was wondering if you'd like to go to dinner with me tomorrow night? I know this great Italian restaurant." He's asking me out? My thoughts do an about-face but not quick enough as John's face turns into a frightened teenager on the verge of being rejected.

## 21

"Absolutely. To see you go up against Manny again would be great." The fear on his face transforms into a grin—a surprised, happy, triumphant grin, and I catch another glimpse of teenager-John receiving a yes.

"Can I meet you there at seven?" he asks.

"That's great." We grin at each other for a few seconds that should be awkward, but they're not.

"Well, tomorrow's gonna be a big day and I'm keeping you up. I'm kinda glad I did, though," he says.

"I'm glad you did, too." If he only knew how often I stay up the entire night looking for Afghani insurgents I'll most likely never find. I shove the thought aside. "I hope tomorrow goes well," I add.

"It will end well," he says.

"Seeing Manny ignore you again will be the perfect ending to the day." We both laugh and then say goodnight. I'm still sitting on the floor, the fan blowing on me as I stare at my phone. A few weeks ago, I would have never believed I would look forward to a date with John Leeman of all people. But I am, and it's a feeling I haven't had in a very long time.

I get up and head to the shower.

MY SHOWER WAS DELAYED, though. I got a call from Nadine.

"You did it, kiddo," she said. I tip my head back and close my eyes. Her sure face topped with spiky silver hair and ever-present red reading glasses on the end of her nose fills my mind. There's a muffled exchange and Neal's voice comes through the line.

"You better believe she did. She was great," he says. They continue back and forth, their exclamations crowding the one line much like proud parents. I squeezed in a thank-you here and there along with a brief reminder that I didn't do this assignment single-handedly. I don't know if they heard me, though. This lopsided conversation went on about ten minutes when father-Neal turned into boss-Neal and reminded me I had an early morning and for me to get to bed.

Just a few seconds after I hung up, I got a FaceTime conference call from Eva, Denise and Gina, their elated faces filling the screen of my phone. We've all worked so hard to have U-Tap taken seriously by the Agency—to prove ourselves—and it has finally happened. It was doubly sweet to see what looked like closure on Eva's face.

When I told them that John had called me to convey the news and that we ended up FaceTiming with Olivia, they went silent. The beaming smiles of anticipation on their faces spoke louder than any words. When I told them John had asked me out to dinner, they exploded with questions and comments.

"It's been a few years since his divorce; it makes sense he would want to date again. And being a single parent is no easy thing, even if John's mother is living there with them," Eva said.

"Did you feel a connection to him? A spark of attraction? He seemed so calm on assignment. Is he the oldest in his family?" Denise asked, not waiting for answers.

"So, y'all looked like this when you were FaceTiming? This is how ya looked when that beautiful Bondman asked you out on a date?" Gina says, pausing long enough to purse her lips. "I know ya have to wear those ugly agency suits, but you have got to step up your game on the hair tomorrow. You hear me?" Gina said.

I haven't laughed so hard in a long, long time and I'm still laughing this morning as I drive to headquarters. I *am* wearing one of my "ugly" agency suits, but I spent some extra time with the blow dryer and curling iron. There will be a definite contrast between last night's sweaty ponytail and today's loose curls with part of it pulled back. Hopefully, Gina will approve. I also hope John notices.

I shake my head at how silly that seems. I'm a thirty-one-year-old experienced CIA officer, why should I care what John thinks about my hair? *It's not silly*, says the voice in my head, and I allow the words to remain.

I park as close as I can to the entrance, giving the morning humidity as little chance as possible of turning my hair into a frizzy mess by the time I get inside.

There are extra chairs in the conference room and donuts, pastries, juice, and coffee cover the long table—the CIA's answer to a morning celebration. The tech guys are here and are putting a good-sized dent in the food. I see Eva, Gina, and Denise across the room and notice their appraisal of me as I grab a bottle of juice. After a surprisingly good night's sleep, the one cup of coffee I had at home has me alert.

I nonchalantly scan the room for John, but don't see him or Neal.

"He's not here yet," Denise says as she and the rest of the team join me.

"I have no idea who you're talking about." The happiness of last evening is still with me—the success of our assignment and John asking me to dinner—and I can't help but tease. Denise gives me a knowing smile.

"Ya look beautiful," Gina says as I watch her dissect my hair. Eva picks up an apple fritter, tears it in half, and gives me the largest half. It's still warm and I take a big bite, enjoying the cinnamon-apple-sweetness as it works through my senses.

"Good morning," comes a familiar voice from behind me. My eyes expand in panic. Why did I take such a big bite? My mouth is so full I can't utter a sound without spewing fritter. And there's no way to chew and swallow this enormous bite in a few seconds, though I'm desperately trying.

I do the only thing I can and turn around to face John. I feel something by my arm, look down and see a napkin fluttering by my hand—Gina's not-so-discreet way of telling me to wipe my face. I do, and to my horror see small bits of fritter and smudges of icing on the napkin. I force down enough to risk a response.

"Good morning," I manage. John shows no acknowledgment of my mouth covered and bulging with fritter. Besides being trained to not show emotion, I'm coming to believe

John is too well mannered to acknowledge something like this. Neal, who must have entered with John, saves me from further embarrassment.

"Good morning. Everyone take a seat. I think our show is just about to start." Chuckles float through the room along with the sound of chairs moving.

"That was smooth," Gina says under her breath as she sits to my left. Eva and Denise sit to my right. I could sit up front with John and Neal but opted to sit with my team. John takes a seat next to Neal, giving me a fritter-free moment to notice how good he looks. Though stunning in his suit, an image of him, hair partially wet and wearing a T-shirt, goes across my mind and I smile.

"Yep. You're going out with that tonight," Eva whispers, and I hear Denise snicker. Nothing gets past these women.

"I just want to take a second and give credit to the person who came up with the idea for this assignment. Officer Ross, thank you." Heads snap around toward me and I see John's eyebrows raise. I knew Neal would eventually do this, but I'm still humbled by the credit—something any of us rarely receive. "It's this kind of creative thinking that will change the face of human intelligence," Neal continues.

"Well, thank you. But it's these women who deserve credit, for believing in my idea. And it was these amazing technicians who made it happen." There was a muffled cheer from the tech guys because most of their mouths are full. The room became instantly silent, though, as the screens come to life, one showing Deputy Thompson and another showing several members of a SWAT team.

22
_____

"Good morning, Officer Gutierrez," Neal says to the SWAT officer standing closest to the camera. I'm sure after all the training that's been going on, Neal knows all their names and can recognize each with their equipment on.

"Good morning. My team is ready, along with the Deputy US Marshals. All vehicles are in position. And from our surveillance, we've confirmed that Garza's men are in the area. We're pretty sure they're planning an attack in the long stretch, which is where my team is positioned. We have more teams at secondary positions."

I look left at Gina, then right at Eva and Denise. This is the spot we all agreed would be the prime spot for an ambush. Garza's men saw it the same way. *Your instincts are right*, says the voice in my head. But they weren't right nine months ago, and Nahla's dead. I close my eyes for a second and give my head a shake.

Eva lays her hand on my forearm. "You okay?" I nod and smile. Her hand and gaze remain on me a few beats too long.

Neal turns to the screen showing Deputy Thompson, and crowded around Thompson are the deputies that helped him yesterday. "Deputy Thompson, I think you and your deputies will enjoy this." Smiles fill the screen.

"We can't wait," Thompson replies.

"Great. Let's go," Neal says. All the SWAT officers give a tight nod and take off in different directions. The footage will rotate from the cameras on the SWAT officers to drones to the deputies positioned outside the prison. There are some operational officers who are tech-trained running the drones and all the remote-control equipment from the prison. No one from yesterday is present in case Garza's men or prison connections saw them.

The drone footage comes on the screen, showing an increasingly closer view of four black SUVs, two in front and two in back of an armored truck. It's a sunny day and the ashen-gray of the prison walls make the SUVs look even shinier.

"I don't think we could announce a prisoner transport any louder," John says.

"The only thing louder than that is a line a school buses at three in the afternoon," Gina says. Laughter rolls through the room. She's right. We might as well hang a sign on one of the SUVs saying, "Hey, Garza Cartel, we got your man right here. Come and get him," which we hope is exactly what they do. I fold my arms across my chest, satisfied with how no one gave Eva and our minivan a second glance yesterday.

We watch as the line of vehicles slowly roll through the gates and pull up to the third building. Deputies in Kevlar vests emerge from the vehicles. They bustle around, shouting, making a show of it. The armored truck parks so close to the door in the prison wall, all that's visible is a flash of orange and a mop of hair moving through the prison door into the armored truck. Then everyone gets in their designated vehicle. The only sound is the tires munching the gravel as the caravan drives past buildings two and one and through the gates.

"Everyone is in position and the equipment is up and functioning," says Gutierrez. There's a collective exhale throughout the room and a few of the tech guys silently high-five each other. I grab Gina's hand and give it a squeeze. "We're in position at the possible ambush site and have a visual on Garza's men." My heart pounds. This is going to work and with a high likelihood of no casualties.

The drone elevates, giving us a visual of the entire caravan pulling through the outer gate. They drive at a steady forty miles-per-hour, providing the SWAT team an exact arrival time at the possible ambush site. "Six minutes and counting," says Gutierrez. I swallow and watch as the drone draws closer, allowing us to see the heads of the deputies inside the SUV. They appear to be scanning the area and talking to each other.

"Three minutes," says Gutierrez. One screen changes to the camera he is wearing. The SWAT team have positioned themselves behind a moveable false front of small trees and shrubs just at the edge of the possible ambush site. By moving it inches at a time, they can close in on a target undetected. The other teams are hiding behind similar camouflage throughout the long stretch in case Garza's men have a Plan B.

I stand, my thighs cutting into the edge of the table. My team joins me. This could be a big payoff and I don't want to miss a thing. A part of me wishes I was there, in the action. Most spies don't get to have a moment like this. I glance at

John and Neal. Their bodies are tense, leaning forward on the balls of their feet, and I wonder if they, too, wish they were inching their way toward the enemy.

"Thirty seconds." I see the first two SUVs emerge from the forested area, then the armored truck followed by the last two SUVs. For two beats, the entire caravan is visible in one long line. And then everything explodes.

## 23

F lames engulf the first and last SUV. Probably
grenade launchers. Two seconds later, the drone
gives us an image like nothing I've ever seen. Rising
like demons and bringing with them chunks of the forest
floor are at least forty men in ghillie suits armed with auto-
matic weapons. Where did they get these elaborate suits, so
perfectly matching the trees and shrubs around them?
Someone studied, crafted, and produced them. Who behind
the gray walls of the prison orchestrated this?

With guns aimed, the bracken-covered demons
approach the armored truck and remaining SUVs. They
seem unfazed by the burning SUVs. But when no panicked
survivors emerge from the two remaining vehicles, we
witness the first hint of confusion.

One screen switches to one SWAT officer on the east side
of the road, another screen to an officer on the west side. We
hear the crunch of the forest floor under their boots as they
slowly move in behind the confused cartel men.

One cartel man screams something, walks up to the

second SUV, and yanks the door open. All of them jump back and aim their guns. The SWAT teams are now close enough for us to hear the cartel's confused commands. Eva chuckles under her breath.

A group of cartel men on the west side carefully approach the driver-side door of the third SUV. A hand emerges from a ghillie suit and pulls the door open. They all jump back, screaming. One pulls a necklace out from under his suit and kisses what I assume to be a cross. I can make out the names of a few saints.

Screaming commands fill the air. Several cartel men go to the back of the armored truck and shoot at the doors until they swing open. That's when I see it—the fraction of a second when they realize they've been caught. It goes beyond body language and expressions. There's an energy that rolls through the air, even this far away. The women next to me are nodding. They know this fraction of a second, they just learned it in different ways.

I've learned to respect this fraction of a second, to anticipate it and plan how I'll respond when it comes. It's great to be on the winning side of it, like now. But to be where the cartel men are will turn you inside out. Nahla fills my mind, but I push the image away. The SWAT team understands this fraction of a second. They train relentlessly for it, which is why they're standing a few yards away when the cartel men turn and try to run.

A few shots are fired, but they appear to reach no human target. There's yelling and commotion on the screens, but it's not long before we have a visual of all the cartel men in handcuffs and sitting on the ground. I can make out some of what the cartel men are yelling, but Eva understands it all and translates some for me. Clearly, they can't believe what they saw inside the SUVs.

What they saw is one of the best spy tools to come out of the Cold War. Each seat that was supposedly occupied by a deputy or officer was, instead, occupied by a jack-in-the-box, or JIB as they're known by the Agency. A JIB consists of a box supporting an inflatable duplicate of each person from the waist up. They are masterfully lifelike and can move via remote control to appear to be looking out the window or talking to another "person" in the vehicle.

As the caravan slowly drove past each building on its way out of the prison, no one saw the deputies, officers and the Lupe-look-alike drop and roll out of the moving vehicles—a classic spy maneuver. No vehicles slowed down, no flash of brake lights to indicate anything suspect taking place. And each person released the lever to inflate their JIB double before hitting the ground and rolling into a side door of one of the prison buildings. It takes perfect timing, but these men have been practicing nonstop and pulled it off without a hitch. The only thing in the armored vehicle was an orange jumpsuit and a wig matching Lupe's massive head of hair.

"We'll search the surrounding areas, but we believe we have all of Garza's men in custody," Gutierrez says. Everyone is standing in the conference room. Thompson and his deputies are standing and applauding. My eyes keep moving from one screen to the next, showing ghillie-suited men lying face down on the ground, their hands cuffed behind their backs. It's an amazing sight. "We'll be sending them your way," Gutierrez adds.

"Great job. That's a beautiful sight," Neal says. Gutierrez gives us a brilliant smile as we all applaud. And then the screens go blank.

I turn and hug each woman, overcome with gratitude. We did it, and the only things lost were two SUVs and some JIBs.

TEN OF GARZA'S men were quick to talk, giving the names of several people in Garza's employ, including prison guards. It's a giant win for law enforcement agencies and the CIA, and it feels amazing to be a part of it. Afghanistan and all that happened there seems far away tonight. Maybe I still *can* do this job.

And now I get to have dinner at Manny's with John. I'm wearing a dress tonight, not an "ugly" agency skirt and blouse, but a pretty summer dress with sandals. My mother loved to sew and always had me wear one of her creations when we went to Manny's. And he never failed to comment on how pretty I looked. I felt special going to Manny's and tonight is no different.

I don't have many dresses now, but the one I'm wearing is my favorite—a pale blue cotton sheath that hits just at the knee. The feel of the hem against my legs brings back memories of my mom pinning up dresses on me to hem, holding the fold of the fabric against the middle of my kneecap to measure. It's sleeveless and feels cool compared to what I wear every day to work. A few more curls in my hair, some silver hoop earrings, and I'm ready. My mom would be pleased.

I spot a parking space less than a half a block down from Manny's and quickly swing my Tahoe in. I don't want to walk very far and give the humidity a chance to ruin the hard work I put in on my hair, not to mention sweating. Gratefully, the evening has cooled off a little.

The pace of my heart increases. John's waiting out front. I haven't been on a date in a while—years, really. There were a few guys during college but I never let the relationships go too far. I'm sure it was the trust thing the CIA counselor talked about. When I signed on with the Agency, my life became way too complicated for a relationship. How could I have a boyfriend while on an overseas assignment?

John's wearing a pale green button-up shirt with gray dress pants and looks amazing. I'm a few yards away and catch a whiff of his cologne. He has his back to me and he's talking on his phone. I stop and wait, not wanting to interrupt him. He's talking to someone about Olivia.

"Okay. Put her on," he says. "Yes, sweetheart, I'm having dinner with Kate-with-the-pretty-eyes." He pauses for a few seconds and I'm close enough to hear a loud, high-pitched voice on the other end. A voice that doesn't sound too happy. "I'm sorry, honey," John says.

## 24

I clutch my small purse as panic churns my stomach. Did it upset Olivia that her dad was going out? Was it too soon to introduce another woman into her life? She seemed to be okay with me when we FaceTimed, but she's had time to think about me, maybe connect the dots to something that makes her feel uncomfortable.

"Yes, Miss Kate likes you. And yes, she would want you to take her to dinner instead of me. But I'm taking Kate to dinner tonight." The panic in my stomach evaporates and I snort-laugh. John quickly turns around and his eyes grow big at the sight of me. It feels good to be taking him off guard for a change.

He smiles while he holds my gaze and listens to Olivia's nonstop talking. He has to repeat her name a few times before she quiets and listens to him. "Would you like to say hi to Miss Kate? She just walked up." He barely had the words out of his mouth before squeals come from his phone. Laughing, he hands his phone to me. It's warm against my cheek and smells like him.

"Hi, Olivia."

"Hi, Miss Kate. Why can't I go to dinner with you?" John hears her question and laughs at what I'm sure registers as panic on my face.

"Well, I never learned good table manners." After the apple fritter incident, it was the first thing I could think of.

"You didn't?"

"No. And your dad needs to teach me some manners before I can have dinner with you."

"Oh. So, you chew with your mouth open and stuff like that?" John is laughing harder but, thankfully, steps away so Olivia can't hear him and question what I'm saying.

"That's right. And I use my hand instead of a fork and I don't wipe my mouth with my napkin." I inwardly wince because part of this is true.

"Wow. My dad will help you. But I would still have dinner with you even if your manners are bad."

"Thanks. You know what? He promised to buy me a cannoli if I do well. Should I have him get an extra one for you?"

"Yeah! I love cannolis. My grandma makes them." I remember that John's mom is most likely standing next to Olivia and hearing this exchange. I hope she's okay with my diversion tactic. John motions for me to give him the phone back.

"Here's your dad. I'm going to try my hardest tonight. Wish me luck."

"Good luck. And if you don't like something, don't spit it out on your plate. Have my dad help you spit it into a paper towel and then he'll throw it away."

"Thanks. I'll do that," I say, doing my best to not laugh, and hand the phone to a red-faced John. He listens to another stream of words I can't make out, mainly because I'm trying to stifle laughter.

"I don't know how Miss Kate got so big and no one taught her manners. I'll find out tonight, okay? Now you can watch one more episode of Paw Patrol and Grandma will read you a story and then it's lights out." I hear a little whining and what sounds like a consent. "I love you, too, sweetheart. Now put Grandma back on."

A woman's voice chuckles on the other end. "I told her one episode of Paw Patrol and one story, then lights out." Her voice is faint but has a kind tone. John slowly smiles. "Yeah. It was a great idea. I'll tell her. Thanks, Mom. I love you, too. Bye."

He taps the red button, puts the phone in his pants pocket and then takes my hand. "Come here," he says and pulls me into a hug. In one move I'm against him, my arms around his chest, my face inches from his neck. His skin smells of soap and cologne. It's been so long since I've been close like this to man. "Thank you. That was some fast thinking," he says, his mouth inches from my ear.

The feel of him so close and so unexpected takes my words, so I nod against his shoulder. His hands move from my back to my upper arms. My eyes close for a second as the warmth of his touch moves down my arms. He pulls me away enough to see his face. "And my mom thinks you're a genius."

We both laugh, then jump apart as the door to Manny's swings open, giving the bell on the door a startling jingle.

"You two gonna just stand out here all night or are you gonna come in and eat?" Manny asks, giving us an irritated look. Manny has probably been watching this entire scene and it may not help Manny's opinion of John.

"Eat," both John and I say. Manny's face lights up and he holds the door wide open for us to enter.

"Well, then get in here, would ya?"

Manny seats us in the same booth we had before, and he's ignoring John just like he did before. I'm sure whatever bit of respect John earned last time he lost when Manny saw him hug me. And maybe me, for hugging John back because Manny says nothing about my dress. John lets me have the side of the booth with the view of the door again. I toss my purse against the wall and using both hands, "slide" in smoother this time.

"I'll get you some water and menus," Manny says, facing me.

"Manny, we don't need menus. How about you just take care of us tonight? I'm sure you know what Kate loves. Is that okay with you?" John asks, turning toward me. I give him a slow, knowing smile because John Leeman just did a very smart thing. If there's one thing Manny Russo loves, it's feeding people what *he* wants to feed them.

"Okay," Manny says, turning toward John. "You want me to take care of you? You hungry?"

"I'm hungry," John says and then looks at me.

"I'm hungry," I add.

"Okay. I'll take care of you and you'll love it."

"My only request is I promised my little girl I'd bring her some cannolis. If I could get an order to go, that would be great." The look on Manny's face brinks on idol worship.

"You got it. You know, when Kate was just this high," he raises his hand to the area of his midsection where his waist would be, "her mom would bring her here, dressed in a beautiful dress like she is tonight and always ask for the same thing." He looks at me, raising his eyebrows.

"Spaghetti and meatballs," I say, finishing his sentence. Manny explodes with laughter, and every inch of his meaty face exudes delight.

"Yeah. Spaghetti and meatballs. I know Kate's favorite. And I'll take good care of you. It's John, right?"

"Yes. John Leeman."

"And your daughter's name is?"

"Olivia."

"Ah, that's a beautiful name. She'll love my cannolis, you'll see." Manny thumps John's side of the table twice with his huge fingers, pivots like a dancer, and heads to the kitchen. John's in with Manny.

"I hope you really *are* hungry because we're about to have an enormous dinner," I say. John smiles and looks so handsome my pulse sounds loudly in my ears.

"I'm hungry," he says and holds my eyes for a few seconds. "You look beautiful, Kate."

I blink. How can he think I'm beautiful? I've hidden in huts for days without bathing, crawled through filthy, reeking places to gather intel. I watched people die, people I know, and had to walk away like they were strangers. I'm not beautiful.

Manny appears at our table as if from nowhere, with a tray filled with drinks, a warm round loaf of bread, and several dipping sauces. He explains each sauce—meaty red sauce which he always refers to as Sunday gravy, olive oil with spices, and two kinds of pesto—and I focus on this like he's explaining my next CIA assignment. It brings me back to the moment and away from John's compliment. Manny vanishes back to the kitchen.

There's no knife with the bread. There never has been

here. I pick up the loaf, rip off a chunk, and hand it to John. "Bread is to be torn. Manny's rules of eating."

"Good to know," he says, taking it. He rips a smaller piece off and tries the olive oil. "I've only had sandwiches here, so hopefully I didn't break any rules."

I dip my bread in the red sauce and take a bite. It's sweet and spicy—delicious. I slide my cloth napkin out from under my silverware and wipe my hands, then lay it across my lap.

"I was going to mention something about using your napkin, but you seem to pick up the manners pretty well," John says as he does the same with his napkin. I laugh, remembering the *real* purpose of this date.

"I worried for a second that Olivia may feel uncomfortable with you taking me to dinner." John swallows a bit of bread dipped in one of the pesto sauces while shaking his head.

"No. Quite the other way around, as you found out. She hasn't stopped talking about you since the other night."

"She seems to have a mind of her own."

"That's a nice way of saying she's stubborn and just a little spoiled. But I want her to grow up to be a strong woman."

"I bet your mom loves having time with her. A lot of grandparents don't have that." A wave of sadness goes through me remembering the few fuzzy memories of my mom's deceased parents. Somewhere in Iraq are Ammar Rasheed's parents that I'll never know.

"Oh, she loves it. Olivia is her only grandchild. My younger sister hasn't married yet." I try to shut off my spy-mind with friends and family, but sometimes it's hard. From what John just told me, his family values are such that having children happens after marriage—a value I hold. It also makes me wonder even more about his divorce. But that's his story to tell when he wants to tell it. The sister seems a safe place to go.

"What's her name?" I read it in his file but can't remember.

"Caroline. She lives in Dallas. She's an ICU nurse and just started dating a doctor at the hospital where she works —which means I'm gonna have to do a serious background check on this guy and maybe go intimidate him with some Agency lingo or something."

"You could have Manny do that for you." And I tell him about my frightened prom date. We're both laughing when Manny appears at our table. We've only made it through half of the bread but he brings us more, along with heaping plates of lasagna, fettuccini in clam sauce and, of course, spaghetti and meatballs. He puts an empty dinner plate in front of each of us.

"I did extra so you can share." He gives us both a commanding look and then turns to me. "I know you like the spaghetti, but you could use some lasagna, too. You looking scrawny." I exhale and mentally add some more miles to my runs for the next week. I raise my eyebrows and nod. What else can I do?

"This looks so good. Thank you, Manny," I say, scooping a serving a lasagna onto my plate. Manny appears assured I won't be wasting away and smiles.

"It smells amazing," John says. Manny gives him a head bob, finger-taps our table twice, and then glides through the surrounding tables to seat a couple who just came in. John takes his first bite of lasagna and closes his eyes. I smile through my first bite and revel from sharing something you love with someone and seeing that they love it, too. "This is really some of the best Italian food I've ever had," he says after a few more bites.

"I'm glad. Sometimes I wonder if I love something just because it's a happy memory from childhood or because it's actually good."

"Well, this is great. But I know what you mean. Childhood memories are a powerful thing. I worry about what memories Olivia will have with the divorce." An awkward pause settles between us.

"It sounds like her dad and grandma create some wonderful memories with her." I really want to know something, anything about his ex-wife. Is she the reason his eyes are sagging with sadness again? And is Olivia safe?

"That's kind of you to say. I mainly worry about Olivia's relationship with her mother. Clare, my ex-wife, has traveled a lot for work over the summer so they haven't had much time together lately. Her traveling will end soon, so maybe she'll be able to see more of her mom." I make a mental note for Gina to do her deep-dive internet magic on Clare and her summer travels. As badly as I want to know more about Clare, I want John to smile again.

"So, some of Lupe's men talked."

"They talked," he says, his lips curving around a bite of linguini. Neal caught me just as I was leaving the office and told me the intel from the cartel men confirmed what Lupe told us on the ride from the prison. "Which reminds me. I want to know how this prison transfer was your idea." I hoped he would ask me this.

"It was really Neal's wife, Nadine, and me. I was at their home for dinner one night."

I was practically living with them after my mom died and

barely functioning from my sudden return from Afghanistan. But that's not exactly first-date stuff. "We were watching a crime drama and frustrated because it was taking forever to find the bad guys. Thinking out loud, I commented that if it were up to a mom to find the bad guys, they would have it done."

"I believe that," he says, twirling some spaghetti on his fork.

"Yes. And it would happen even faster if the moms were ticked-off about something." John laughs and chokes a little on his bite of spaghetti. "The real power in this idea is that moms are pretty much invisible. They're the last people anyone expects, so they make the perfect spies."

"Genius is what it is." I want to let this compliment in but I've made so many mistakes, costly mistakes, I only allow it to hit the surface.

We talk about the transfer and some great tradecraft the team has gained. It's easy to talk to John, which really means John listens well while I ramble on about my team.

"It took a lot of guts to ride around with Lupe in a mini-van," he says when I give him a chance.

"Yeah. And the ability to handle terrible smells." Manny chose that moment to appear at our table. "Just work stuff, Manny. Not your food."

"Good to know." He looks a little confused, probably wondering what terrible smells there are to endure at the state department, where he believes I work. "How about I take these dishes and divide them into two doggie bags and package up some cannolis for the both of you?" I think Manny is the only person alive who still uses the phrase "doggie bags."

John and I both agree. I don't think I can put one more

bite in my mouth, no matter how delicious the food is. Manny leaves the check and gathers up the dishes. I feel bad that there aren't larger dents in each dish, but the portions he gave us were huge even for Manny. At least John's mom won't have to cook tomorrow, or maybe even the next day.

The evening air is cool and spicy. Is it a hint of fall or just wishful thinking? John must have given Manny a generous tip, because not only did Manny hug me, he hugged John too and made him promise to bring Olivia with him next time. Manny is sure she'll love the spaghetti and meatballs.

John carries the bagged to-go boxes—each larger than our original orders—as he walks me to my Tahoe. I didn't notice, but I parked two cars down from his Chevy Silverado truck. I guess I was a little distracted walking to Manny's. The streetlights wave off the silver hood. John puts his food in the passenger side and locks the door.

"Let's put your food in your car and walk a bit. It's cool enough I think it'll be okay for a few minutes." I unlock my Tahoe and he puts the bag in the back seat.

I try to push away all the questions that are elbowing their way into my brain—where is this thing with John going? Is this a thing? It feels like a thing, or am I imagining it. *Relax and enjoy the moment,* the voice in my head tells me. But all my training has taught me to be three moves ahead.

J ohn shuts the door of my Tahoe and I click the lock but hold the button on the fob too long and the horn honks, which makes me jump and laugh. I'm an idiot. "Yeah, I'm a six-year-old," I say, trying to cover it up. He just grins and takes my hand.

"Let's walk down this way," he says, leading me toward a path through what appears to be a small garden in between two buildings.

Walking next to John, his arm moving against mine with each stride, our palms touching, awakens a part of me that's been asleep for a long time. Since my mother died, I've had such little equal human contact I had forgotten the feel of it. Not the forceful blow of combat where one wins and one loses. And not the mournful hug of someone offering condolences—they giving and you taking on the one-way path of pity. It's the equal touch between two people who are both taking and receiving.

With John holding my hand, our fingers woven together like equal strands of a rope, I feel safe. The questions in my brain evaporate and the voice in my head says, *See*?

The light from quaint lamp posts expose patches of fuchsia zinnias, blush dahlias, and sun-yellow daisies. Hostas, with dinner-plate-size leaves, wreath the base of trees that drape over the path. It's breathtaking. Why have I never noticed this garden before? I have to come back in the daytime.

We stop in front of a bench and John pulls me down to sit. A large hydrangea bush in full bloom is our backrest. A tickle skips up my arm as my elbow brushes against a feathery cluster of pink blooms. Our eyes connect and relax into a comfortable gaze that would probably be weird for anyone else but us.

"I have to be honest with you," John says, "Neal asked me to spend some time with you so you'd feel comfortable working with me." Any "define the relationship" conversation starter normally makes me squirm. Not now, though. Not with how John's looking at me.

"He asked me to do the same." I leave out some major details of my conversation—more like argument—with Neal.

"I know. He told me. But after the first time at Manny's, I wanted to spend more time with you. Not just for work, but normal time." He stutters over the last few words. It takes guts for him to say this, and the awkwardness is touching and real. I just honked my horn and thought it was funny. I know all about awkward.

"You would like to be my friend," I say. His shoulders slump a little and he exhales.

"Yes. I'd very much like to be your friend. I haven't dated or anything since my divorce. I didn't want to bring any more change into Livvy's life and, I don't know, I didn't really want to date." He pauses and looks across the path. "When I'm with you, I feel safe. I haven't felt safe for a long time."

As much as I would like to ask him why, I don't. Instead, I give his hand a squeeze. "I'll be your friend. And I understand the safe thing. I haven't exactly been the poster child of emotional strength for the last nine months. And apparently I have horrible table manners." We both laugh at that, the easy laugh of people on the same page.

We stand at the same time and start walking toward the street. I don't want to leave this secluded Eden and say as much. "I never knew this was here. Did you?"

"This is one of my favorite places. Some gardening group that wanted to give back to the city put it in a few years ago. I come here during the day sometimes, when I can get away."

"I must come and see this in daylight."

"It's beautiful. Maybe we can get a doggie bag from Manny's and have lunch here." I chuckle at the phrase.

"Sounds great. I think Manny is going to resurrect the phrase 'doggie bag.' He's the only person I know who uses it."

"I think you're right." We're at my Tahoe, but I make no move to get my keys out of my purse. John is still holding my hand. He's never let go of it. "Will you come spend Sunday afternoon with us?"

My heart jumps into my throat. By "us" he must mean his mom and Olivia. Am I ready for this? His eyes search my face but stop when I smile. "I'd love to. You sure that will be okay with everyone?"

"My mom would love to meet you. And I'm supposed to give you this." He lets go of my hand and pulls out a folded piece of paper from his pants pocket and hands it to me. With little prodding, the creases fall open.

By the streetlight, I see a crayon drawing in multiple colors—a house with a four-year-old's version of three humans standing next to it. One human, a man, is large with dark, short hair. Another, a woman, is slightly smaller with long dark hair and aqua-blue eyes. And the third, a girl, is small with brown hair and brown eyes. Stars fill the remaining space on the paper. "This is Olivia's invitation for you to come on Sunday."

Each star drawn with a different color, each outlined space carefully filled in, each fold Olivia creased over and over shows me this invitation is precious to her. I run my fingers across the waxy crayon lines. I can't pull my eyes from the paper.

"So, she's okay with me coming," I finally say.

"She's more than okay. So am I." I look up to see his eyes watching me.

"Well, what time should I be there?"

"I better ask my mom, since she's cooking. We get out of church at noon, so after that. I'll text you, along with our address." Guilt pinches my chest. Neal mentioned that John attends the same Christian church he and Nadine do, the same church my mom and I went to. I haven't been since I returned from Afghanistan, though. I look back down at the picture.

"This is really sweet." My voice cracks on the last word. Before I can look back up, John has his arms around me and pulls me into a hug.

"You're sweet." I feel his breath against my hair. The closeness of him makes me forget things—where I am, what's going on around me. For a spy, that's a big deal. But

I'm okay with it. The word "sweet," though, is all wrong. The feather-like petals of the hydrangea are sweet, not me. All the hard, ugly things I've had to do grate against such a delicate word.

He pulls away and smiles. "Thank you for tonight and for being my friend." His eyes tell me he means it.

"Thank you. Tell Olivia I'll see her Sunday." We walk around to the driver's side as I push unlock on my key fob. He opens the door for me and shuts it once I'm in, then stands on the sidewalk as I drive away.

When I get home, the first thing I do is put Olivia's invitation on my fridge. As soon as I attach it with a magnet, it becomes the center of this space. It pulls on my heart and as I move about, getting ready for bed, I keep finding reasons to walk past the kitchen so I can glance at it.

I'VE SPENT the last forty-eight hours stressing about what it will be like going to John's home and meeting his mom. Of all the dangerous and frightening places I've had to enter—most pretending to be someone else—I'm now anxious about going to the home of a fellow officer and meeting his mom and darling daughter.

John texted me the morning after our dinner at Manny's, thanked me for a lovely evening, and asked if I'd come at two on Sunday. It took me a while, but I finally decided on a pair of dressy jeans and a lavender peasant blouse. I left in time to stop and get a bouquet of pink hydrangeas for John's mom and a Paw Patrol coloring box for Olivia, complete with crayons, colored pencils, stickers, stamps, and several coloring books and pads.

The street they live in South Kensington appears to be a neighborhood of families—children are playing, bikes and toys are in yards, chalk drawings here and there on the sidewalks. It's not postcard perfect, but if I were a child, I'd want to live here. It makes me happy that this is where Olivia spends at least part of her life.

I'm surprised when I pull up to the front of John's home, to see that it's just a normal-looking home—single story with a porch. Do I expect all men who look like male models to live in chrome-filled pent houses? I take a few deep breaths before I open the Tahoe door and get out. I'm seriously wondering if I know how to do normal anymore.

With flowers and coloring box in hand and my purse slung over my shoulder, I head up the front walk. The flower beds are ablaze with color and hanging pots dripping flowers line the porch. Someone here likes to garden.

When I'm about three feet away, the front door swings open and Olivia comes flying out.

# 26

"**Y**ou came! You came!" Olivia's dancing and flinging her hands up and down. I squat down in front of her. The photo Gina showed us was recent: it looked exactly like the little girl in front of me, right down to the missing tooth.

"Of course I came. Thank you for such a beautiful invitation. I put it on my fridge. And I brought you something." I hand her the coloring box. She takes it in both her hands and studies it for a few seconds. And then she looks at me and smiles.

"Thank you," she says. I don't feel anxious anymore. In fact, all that matters in this moment is that this little girl in front of me is smiling.

I stand and meet the pleased face of her father. He's in jeans and a short-sleeved navy crewneck that exposes the muscles I knew were there but haven't seen until now.

"I'm happy you're here. Come and meet my mom." I follow him in the house with Olivia beside me, taking long and short steps as she stares at her gift instead of where she's stepping. In the entry is a small table with a white milk-glass vase filled with a wild array of flowers and ivy. Hanging on the wall behind the vase is a picture of a handsome middle-aged man—John's father who he was named after, a school teacher who died when John was in high school. I see John in his square jaw and kind smile.

We walk from the entryway into a great room with a large open kitchen. My mouth waters at the accumulated smells, both sweet and savory. Scattered across light granite countertops are various utensils—a wooden spoon, a cutting board and knife, and a pair of potholders. In the living area, I recognize the brown sofa from our FaceTime and glance to my left to see the hallway that leads to Olivia's room. A vibrant oriental rug of red, gold, and navy adorns the rough-hewn wooden floors.

Their home feels beautiful and comfortable, tidy but lived in—like you could lie down on the sofa and take a nap. A beautiful woman walks through an open sliding glass door. She has Japanese features, but they are not as distinct as they would be if both her parents had been of Asian descent. I remember John's file listing his grandmother as Japanese and his grandfather American. She has a petite frame, a thick braid draped over her left shoulder and not a wrinkle on her youthful face. The only evidence she is older than John are the strands of gray woven through her braid and the years of life I recognize in her eyes. She doesn't wait for John's introduction.

"Hello, Kate, with the pretty eyes," she says, taking my free hand. "I'm Rose Leeman." Her smile is radiant. Rose Leeman has a very fortunate gene pool, and it's obvious she's passed a good portion of it on to her son.

"It's so nice to meet you. Thank you for having me. These are for you," and hand her the flowers.

"Oh, I love hydrangeas. And the pink is my favorite. Why don't you come and see my garden?" And with that, I'm led into a gardening wonderland. The edges of the huge square yard—what registers as two lots in this neighborhood—are softened with mounds of flowering shrubs including gorgeous pink, blue, and white hydrangeas. Branches of well-placed trees arch their shielding protection over us. Round, sweeping flowerbeds are here and there, and vines roam free. There's a stone walkway leading to a small cottage, which I assume to be Rose's. I'm reminded of an exotic Japanese garden but not so exacting—messier, wilder.

Rose gives me a tour, explaining plants and flowers, asking my opinion on color. I have a limited knowledge but great appreciation for plant life and tell her so, which makes her laugh.

I feel John behind me and turn around. He hands me a glass of iced tea, winks, and then hands his mom a glass too. Without looking at him, Rose takes the glass, not missing a beat in her detailed description of the different ivy.

We eat under the trees on a white linen-covered table adorned with my hydrangeas. The afternoon is pleasant, with a breeze that tosses the branches overhead and swirls the spicy fragrance of gardenias in the air.

We start with chilled cucumber salad and sliced toma-toes. I can tell these vegetables are fresh—there's nothing in the stores that can mimic this flavor—and ask where the vegetable garden is. Rose points out the small greenhouse at the side of the house, masterfully camouflaged with yet another type of ivy.

Chicken breasts stuffed with fresh mozzarella cheese,

sautéed vegetables and rice follow. It's simple but so flavorful and I eat everything on my plate. I notice Olivia eats all her vegetables without encouragement. With Rose as her grandmother, I imagine meals like this are the norm and there's probably little success at fighting it.

Our conversation is easy. Rose tells me about growing up in San Francisco and taking several trips to Japan with her parents to visit family. John has been several times and both are fluent in Japanese. I wonder how many of those trips were Agency assignments. Surely the CIA wouldn't waste his appearance and language skills. Though Rose knows about the CIA, he mentions nothing about work and I'm sure it is to protect Olivia.

I watch John as he talks. He's not putting on a show for me. This is how he lives. Maybe not linen tablecloths and Sunday-like lunch on the lawn every day, but the relationships with his mother and daughter are authentic. I can tell when someone is trying to hide dysfunction, and it doesn't feel like any of that is going on here.

I share a little about growing up in Maryland and some of my favorite historical sites like Richmond and Williamsburg, Virginia. Rose tells me how sorry she is about my mother passing and, like her son, asks to hear what she was like. Olivia, who has finished eating and is exploring her coloring box, looks up at the mention of my mother.

"Did she have pretty eyes, like you?" she asks.

"She did. In fact, everyone always tells me I have her eyes." Olivia looks at me for a few seconds and then pulls colored pencils and paper out of her box.

"I'm going to draw a picture of your mom. What color hair did she had?" She is oblivious to what this does to my heart.

"She had blonde hair and fair skin. I got my tan skin and dark hair from my dad, but my eyes from my mom." Olivia nods and begins drawing, her brows knit together with concentration. A child can tell you a great deal in just a few moments, mainly by what they don't say. All this talk of mothers and Olivia mentions nothing about her own.

I'm not allowed to help clear the table. "Guests don't clean up. It's part of having good manners," Olivia reminds me. As we ate, I noticed her watching me and then give her father an approving look. Perhaps I passed the manners test.

Olivia hands me a clean sheet of paper and lays out the crayons so I can color something with her. John and Rose are busy clearing the table off, and I try to act normal as John leans over me to clear away my dishes. He smells as good as all the flowers combined.

We are engrossed in our coloring—me trying to capture the riot of pink roses arching over the entrance to Rose's cottage and Olivia with what looks like me with blonde hair —when John slides a dish in front of me. "It's not an apple fritter, but it's close." It's a delicious-looking slice of apple pie with a scoop of vanilla ice cream on top. Two seconds pass before the joke registers. I look up into his silently laughing face and I can't help but laugh out loud.

"So, you saw that." I was so hoping he hadn't noticed the fritter incident in the meeting. But that he's been sitting on this, waiting to spring it on me, makes me laugh again.

"I saw it, but it'll be our little secret." As if on cue, Rose puts a dish in front of Olivia and sits down with her own.

"John tells me you love apple fritters. I've never made those, but I can make a decent pie. I hope you like it." I cover the laughter well enough to take a bite of pie and convey how delicious it is. John's thoroughly enjoying himself.

We take our time and enjoy dessert. Olivia eats her pie as if on autopilot while focusing on her drawing. I watch her as she adds a few more stars to the empty spaces and then sets her crayon down. She's done and a look of satisfaction crosses her face. I'm envious of her ability to finish and be satisfied. I'd keep fiddling with it.

"Here's a picture of your mom. When you miss her, you can look at this." Olivia hands me the drawing with childlike certainty on her face—she's sure it will bring me comfort.

"I will. This looks just like her. I'll put it on my fridge when I get home. Thank you." She rests her damp, cool palm on the back of my hand.

"Call me Livvy, like my dad and grandma do." With the elimination of one letter, I'm allowed into a closer circle of her world.

"Livvy it is." She pats my hand a few times and then picks up her spoon to finish eating her pie. John and Rose look at me and I sense the mood change. Are they wondering, now that Olivia has let me closer, if I will hurt her? Can they trust me with this child's already fragile emotions? I keep my eyes on the drawing and let it pass. Words are too cheap to fill this moment. The fruits of my life are of much greater value. I will show them I'm a safe person in Olivia's life for however long I'm allowed in it.

It's best to leave someone's home before the obvious moment to do so presents itself. But I don't want to go. After three hours, the idea that I was ever unsure about coming here seems ridiculous. Being around Rose and Livvy is like being around the best parts of what we call home. Up to this point, John has been a mystery, especially regarding his ex-wife. But now it's more of a question rather than a mystery.

Rose bundles up enough leftovers for me to last at least

three days. She hugs me and thanks me again for the flowers. The smell of earth and the day's cooking is about her, and it makes me want to curl up on the sofa so she can watch over me.

Livvy and John walk me to my Tahoe. The heavy blue of dusk has settled in, but it's still light enough for children to play. Night games we called them growing up, and they were one of the best parts of summer. I see small groups of children gathering on lawns and hear their laughter and dares and I'm thankful Livvy lives part of her life here.

"This afternoon's gone by too quickly," John says. "It's been nice having you here." I want to tell him I haven't been in a home—including my own—where I've felt so at home since my mother died. But I just smile and thank him for having me.

"When will you come back?" Livvy asks. She jerks her body a few times and whines. John rubs his hand over her hair and hums some soothing words. She's so well behaved, it's easy to forget she's only four. Did she miss her normal nap time because of my visit? I hand the leftovers to John and squat down.

"I would love to come back whenever you and your dad invite me. But you know what we could do in the meantime?" Tears have welled up in her eyes, but she focuses on my question. "We can FaceTime. That was fun, wasn't it?" She nods and smiles. I don't want to make any promises to her that puts John in an awkward position. Maybe he doesn't want to invite me over again. But I figured the promise of FaceTiming was safe and could avert a full-blown meltdown. I smile back and she throws her arms around my neck. Her little body jerks as she swallows a few sobs. I let her hug me as long as she wants and after a moment, she lets go. Her skin is warm as my thumb sweeps away tears from her cheeks.

"Your eyes look even bluer at night," she says as she touches the side of my eye with her index finger. I give her another smile.

"You okay now?" I ask. She nods and I stand up. The look of appreciation on John's face makes my heart ache. How could I have ever thought this man didn't love his daughter? He hands me the leftovers, but as I take them, he holds his hand over mine under the container. I take a deep breath. The warmth of his skin runs up my arm.

"Thank you. For everything." His eyes look glossy and for the hundredth time I want to ask who hurt him. How much pain has this little family been through, and who caused it? He gives my hand a squeeze and then reaches around to open the Tahoe's door.

Livvy bounces and waves as I get in, content with the promises I could make her. They both wave as I drive off with food and a picture of my mother on the front seat. When I'm home, I walk in my front door and directly to my fridge. With my purse on my shoulder and leftovers in one hand, I hang Livvy's drawing. It pulls my eyes even more than the first one.

I LURCH AWAKE, then lay completely still. My breath is shaky and although I'm in a tank top and shorts, sweat covers my back. The first explanation my mind comes up with for the pounding is shelling—if you've been near artillery shelling, it becomes number one on a mental list of worst-case scenarios. I'm only slightly relieved when I register the safety of my bedroom and that the pounding is someone at my door. I glance at my phone. It's midnight.

I've made too many enemies to not have a gun in my nightstand. I grab it and my phone and head to the front door. Images of who could be on the other side race through my mind. My finger is on the gun's safety, ready to release it. I force myself to take in a chest-full of air and slowly release it.

I never look through peepholes. As small as that hole is, your enemy can tell when it goes dark—when you are standing on the other side of the door—and shoot you. I keep mine covered at all times.

I skirt my entryway in order to glance out the small space between my window seal and blinds, but before I get there, I hear John's voice.

## 27

M y mind switches mid-thought. Is something wrong with Livvy? Why would John come here, though? And why wouldn't he just call me? The answer to that last question changes the scenario of the problem completely—he doesn't want any traceable evidence of the conversation we're about to have . . . on my doorstep . . . at midnight. My mouth goes dry. This isn't about Livvy.

I swing the door open. John's in work clothes—dark suite, white dress shirt, but his tie hangs loose. Pinch-faced and frightened, he seeks my eyes and holds them. A few seconds pass as I feel us silently ask and answer questions similar to what just went through my head.

"I'll be gone for a few days. I have to leave. Now. When I get back, things could be different."

"Different?"

"At work. There could be some difficult things. Things that could make it hard for you." I narrow my eyes. He's mentally dancing around something he can't tell me, something classified. The words "different," "difficult," and "hard" irritate me. I know all the awful assignments that could stand behind those words. Why am I being handled so carefully? And by John?

"What's going on?" He pinches his lips together and shakes his head.

"I can't tell you, but you'll find out when I get back."

"Then why are you here?" He pauses and looks at me again. Is it fear I see in his eyes? Is he afraid to tell me?

"What you'll find out in a few days may change work, but I don't want it to change this, our friendship. Please, trust me." There's that word—trust. Whatever my face is showing makes John's eyes even more frightened. "Please, trust me, Kate." I sense he's in a hurry, but he remains motionless on my front step.

"You'll tell me everything you can when you get back?" I know how this works. Secrets layered on secrets with only a few people knowing the whole truth. I've lived this life for so long and now, once again, it's personal. Isn't lying always personal? Relief rolls across his face at my request.

And then John does the last thing I expect him to do. He clears the distance between us—the tangible, tingly space ever-present between two people attracted to each other—and kisses me. "Everything I can," he whispers. He's so close, his lips move against mine with each word. For a second, we share one space, the same air and my jumpy, erratic thoughts of a few minutes ago draw together as one. Then he turns and runs to his car, and is gone.

I close and lock the door and then stare at the floor for I don't know how long. What did I just agree to?

My safe space beckons—my crazy room. I flip on the

light and the walls jump at me, busy and complicated against the simple beauty of the day. Pushing the contrast aside, I force my eyes across each wall, seeing but not seeing as flowers and crayons and sliced tomatoes try to elbow their way onto my mental stage. John's words roll as the background dialogue in my mind and my lips are changed by his kiss. I curl them in to hold on to the feeling.

What will be different? Why does anything have to change? Can I do what John asks and trust him? I churn through these thoughts until the gray-dawn comes through the cracks of the blinds. I turn the light off and go take a shower.

JOHN DIDN'T RETURN until Thursday. Neal announced a briefing Wednesday evening for the next morning, saying we'd start as soon as John got in from the airport. The briefing would outline a new assignment for an elated U-Tap team. Because of all the paperwork required for Lupe's transfer, Eva had stayed in Maryland, providing us all with home-cooked Mexican food while staying at Gina's.

I have a standing dinner invitation with both Gina and Denise, especially when Eva is in town and cooking. But I declined this week. I'm so worried about John, I didn't think I'd be good company. Because of what John mentioned— how something may be different—and the classified nature of whatever this is, I don't feel comfortable sharing what he said, not even with U-Tap. And with their amazing mom-spy skills, I wouldn't be able to keep anything about John from them, so I used paperwork as my excuse to keep to myself.

John has arrived and is standing up front with Neal. My

heart pounds against my tight chest. I want to run up to him and scream all the questions that have monopolized my mind since Sunday night. But I have to be cool and act like I know nothing.

There are dark circles under John's eyes and his face is drawn. My chest loosens a little as I consider where he's been and what he's been through. In our line of work, it could almost be anywhere and anything.

My eyes linger on him. I follow his lips as they move, exchanging small talk with an analyst. I catch a whiff of his cologne and inhale. Standing in this large conference room with officers roaming around and tech guys prepping equipment and analysts coming in and out with reports—I know what John Leeman's lips feel like. And I also know I'm going to have to trust him with something "difficult."

Eva, Gina, and Denise come in together. Eva walks on the balls of her feet, Denise carries a full cup holder from Starbucks, and Gina has a pair of pumpkin-orange readers on the end of her nose. My team is ready for work.

"This meeting calls for pumpkin-spice lattes for everyone," Denise says, while she hands each of us a warm cup.

"So, what do you think this is about?" Eva asks. I shrug and take a sip, hoping the action hides my lie. Denise's eyes narrow on me.

"Well, would y'all look at that?" Gina says. My eyebrows raise as I watch three FBI agents walk into the room. One is Agent Maxwell. I purse my lips and exhale. Why are they here? And why Maxwell? The agents step aside, allowing a secretary to go out and close the door. My team and I pull out chairs from the table and sit, but everyone else takes their time finding chairs.

John catches my eye and gives me a slight nod, but there are no smiles between us. My pulse thumps on my neck and I take another sip of latte. Would everyone be quiet and sit down? The sooner we get this meeting started, the sooner I know what's going on with John and his secrets.

"Glad you're all here," Neal says, finally. "I'm grateful to have Officer Leeman and our friends from the FBI joining us. This second assignment for U-Tap will be another outside-the-box kind of assignment, but this time it will be to gather intel—what we spies love to do." A chuckle rumbles through the room. "It will also require, like the Garza prison transfer, the partnership with law enforcement agencies, this time with the FBI."

No chuckles follow this announcement. These two agencies don't always play well together. My curiosity about this "difficult" assignment, that has the potential of changing my friendship with John, just went up a few notches. "I'm going to turn the time over to John, who has the details. And this is all classified. Nothing leaves this room."

John stands and takes Neal's place. His face is pale and his eyes are sagging. I brace myself, knowing John will get right to the point. "We're all familiar with sleeper cells. These terrorists are running the long game. They come to America and invest years, sometimes decades, embedding themselves into our lives. As Neal said, this will be another different assignment, not only because we'll be working with the FBI and U-Tap, but because it's become personal, at least for me." He picks up the screen remote and looks down at it as if it's the last thing on earth he wants to hold. My arms fold over my chest and my hands squeeze into fists. I swallow the saliva that's pooled up in the back of my mouth.

A picture of Clare comes up on the screen—beautiful, smiling, like a model. "We have intel that leads us to believe Clare Leeman, my ex-wife, is a radical jihadist, a part of a sleeper cell, who has recently been activated."

## 28

M y mouth drops open. My ears ring. I can't process the words John just said. His ex-wife is a terrorist? I stare at John and he stares back. And then I look at the table, my hands, the floor, the statue-like women sitting next to me. The dots connect in my mind, all leading to one question I blurt out.

"Is your daughter safe?" Everyone in the room looks at me, but I don't care. My eyes are back on John's and I catch a whisper of a smile cross his lips.

"Olivia is safe for the time being. I know you have many questions. Hopefully, I can answer a few right now, but all we know will be in the files. Clare was born an American citizen, but we've recently learned she has dual citizenship with Afghanistan." A knowing moan goes through the room. In theory, this isn't possible, but we all know in practice, Americans can be Afghani citizens. It's common among terrorists.

"Clare was radicalized during her college years, which means she was radicalized when we married. I had no idea.

She passed all CIA background checks for spouses. Without becoming unduly personal, let this be one more warning of just how thoroughly convincing a radical jihadist can be. I was tricked, and the Agency was tricked." John pauses for a moment. My throat tightens and I try to clear it by coughing. Is there anything as awful as being tricked by someone you trust?

I glance over at the FBI agents. When the meeting began, they were leaning back in their chairs, arms folded across their chests, ready to pick a fight. Now, they sit forward, arms resting on their thighs, eyes drawn up in worry. The safety of a child puts everyone on the same team.

"As you'll read in the file, she works for Harrod and Raynott Financial, an international finance group with clients worldwide, including the Middle East. The company checks out, so, again, it's a part of the long game. This job is the perfect reason to travel, have language skills, and knowledge in big finance. All skills that come in handy as a terrorist. I just assumed they were a part of what she did for work." The sarcasm in his voice is hard to miss.

"Have ya found another passport or ID for her?" Gina asks. I'm wondering the same thing. Though, if she's a highly trained terrorist—one that's been activated—her fake documentation wouldn't be easy to find. And there wouldn't be multiples hidden in a box somewhere like is so often depicted in movies. There's usually just one set because they're much too valuable and difficult to produce.

"No, not yet. If she's traveling for work, she wouldn't need them. But we're sure they'll surface because eventually she *will* need them. She's been out of the country—supposedly for work—for most of the summer, where we feel she was receiving some special training for this activation. According

to the schedule she's given me, her traveling will slow down."
There's an awkward pause where I imagine John working
out Olivia's schedule while acting as if he doesn't know the
mother of his child is a terrorist.

"I'll do some more digging and see what I can find," Gina
says. The words fill the silent space. With what she's gone
through with her own divorce, I know Gina would try to
soften this any way she can. John gives her a nod.

"It was through an in-country Afghani agent that we
learned Clare has been activated. I just returned from a face-
to-face meeting with him." So, this is where John went—to
Afghanistan to find out in person that Clare's a terrorist.
"Unfortunately, we have no actionable intelligence that tells
us what her mission is. Because she's an American citizen,
we've asked the FBI to help us with our surveillance. But
because we also believe she's a terrorist threat, we've been
given the okay to blur the lines a bit. We need some 'invisible' people in her life with some cameras and recording
devices. We need help from U-Tap."

Slow nods come from the three ladies flanking me. This
is why this team was created. Yet, something keeps floating
around in my mind—a question I need to ask but don't want
to. I have so many questions, though, I can't seem to pin this
one down.

"Has Olivia shown any signs of being uncomfortable
with her mom?" Denise asks. She watched her sons be
frightened by gangs for years. She could recognize a frightened child better than any of us.

"Since our divorce a few years ago, Clare has traveled a
lot. There's not the bond that would normally exist between
mother and child. Clare is very controlling and so the time
she and Olivia spend together consists of a full and regi-

mented schedule of activities. Clare allows her to have play dates with other children of people she knows—mainly coworkers." Denise remains quiet. I've seen her do this quit often, when someone doesn't answer her question. She remains calm, but I see a few people squirm.

She nods her head with an encouraging look on her face.

"So, I guess I didn't answer your question, did I?" John asks. Denise smiles and waits. "I haven't picked up any sign that Olivia is frightened, but she's said a few things that make me feel like she can't please her mom."

"That is common with controlling parents," Denise says.

"My mother lives with me and watches Olivia when I'm working. We try to have a more relaxed schedule with free time to play, more like a normal childhood. I hope it helps to undo some pressure Olivia feels when she's with her mother." John sounds defensive and there's another awkward pause.

"Children are so adaptable. It sounds like she has a loving environment with you and your mother," Denise says. I'm sure she's trying to take the edge off his defensiveness. John smiles, but it looks forced.

"So, intel shows Clare isn't acting alone, that there's most likely a group that has been activated. If she's not traveling, she must have contact with them in her day-to-day life. We need to know who she's working with and for what purpose they were activated. We thought we'd put it out to U-Tap and ask your suggestions. Clare lives in Bethesda and takes Olivia to Nithercott Daycare. She's four, so she will start preschool at Jarsdel in a few weeks. The daycare provides transportation to and from preschool."

"Nithercott and Jarsdel? Those are crazy expensive and you have to be on a waiting list almost from the time your child is born," says one of the tech guys who has two small children. I was wondering the same thing. Were John and Clare planning on sending Olivia to these elite childcare places? Even with their combined incomes, it would have been a stretch.

"You're right. We couldn't consider doing this when we were married," John says. "Clare had mentioned nothing about it until a few months ago. And she didn't have any problem getting Olivia in immediately. Another red flag. But if our intel is right, she also has a huge terrorist organization with unlimited funds backing her."

"If Clare lives in Bethesda and works full time, she probably has a housecleaning service." Eva says. "Maids can be pretty invisible, and I know how to clean a house."

"She has Appearance Maid Service that comes in twice a week," Gina says, reading from a page in the file.

"Great idea, Eva. We'll take care of the details and get you on Clare's schedule," Neal says.

"And if Nithercott provides transportation, there's no one more invisible as the mom driving carpool. If I could be the driver taking Olivia to and from Jarsdel, I may get a different read on Olivia and check out some other moms," Denise says.

"That would be perfect," John says while Neal writes notes on a legal pad. My mind is racing, moving from detail to detail regarding Eva's and Denise's roles. They may not be glamorous spying assignments, but the opportunity they will have to gather human intel is tremendous. Whether or not moms realize it, they are always running surveillance—they see the same scenes every day and can spot in a moment if something's off. I'm so preoccupied, I don't hear Neal call my name until Eva nudges my arm.

"Kate. I'd like both you and John to run this assignment. You've earned the right to head U-Tap, but because of the insight John can give us, I think it best to have you two work together." This stings a little, but I agree. Normally, John wouldn't be allowed anywhere near this assignment because of his connection to Clare. But fighting a different enemy requires new tactics. I nod my head in agreement.

"Because you've had so much experience with disguise, I thought you could tail Clare and see where she's really going every day. It would give us another chance to see the cell she's working with."

"Of course," I say. I notice how he doesn't put me with Olivia. She's already seen me, so I have no cover with her like Eva and Denise do. But no one knows this, so he doesn't mention it.

"And Gina, we'll be gathering a lot of intel, not just from U-Tap but from three case officers with agents in Afghanistan. We'll need your magic at organizing all this so Kate and I can sift through it all."

"You got it."

"Of course, you'll have your tech posse and anything you need," John adds. There are a few awkward chuckles at John's attempt at humor. But that's okay. He looks better than when this meeting started—relieved, with more color to his face. It's got to feel good to have support on such a personal and horrible assignment.

That feeling comes back—that there's a question I don't want to look at and keep pushing away. I make myself focus as John tells us we'll meet again in a few days to go over details of our assignments. I'm just turning to talk to Eva when I hear my name.

"Kate, I'll give you some time with your team and then

we need to meet. That sound okay?" John asks. His eyes lock on mine and the kiss we shared just hours ago rolls across my mind. And I know he sees it because I see it roll across his face.

"Sounds good," I answer. I'm going to have to explain some things to my team because they all saw it, too.

## 29

Eva, Denise, Gina and I remain in the conference room for our meeting. I exchange awkward glances with people as they leave. There are no pleasantries to exchange after learning what we just learned. I read Maxwell's lips as he assures John that he and the other agents will do all they can to help him. My mouth is dry and I take a big swallow of my latte.

When we have the room to ourselves, Eva looks at me and folds her arms. Denise is silently waiting. Gina looks like she'll burst if I don't start talking. I tell them about my Sunday afternoon at John's home and his late-night visit to mine. I didn't tell them John kissed me, though. Some things are just mine, but I'm sure they all figured he had by the way he looked at me. I wonder how many others figured it out. John could have hidden that look, but he didn't. In a way, it was flattering.

"No wonder you've been so weird all week," Gina says.

"I would have told you, but I didn't know how much was

classified. And I figured we'd all find out when John returned."

"It's okay," Eva says and gives my arm a squeeze. "We understand this job will require a need-to-know basis sometimes."

"I can't believe that Miss America look-alike is a terrorist," Gina says.

"I can," says Eva and Denise together.

"Who would ever suspect Clare Leeman of being part of a sleeper cell? She's perfect," Denise explains. Eva nods in agreement. They're both right.

"It's the entire premise of U-Tap, just a little too close for me to see," I say. Eva reaches over and gives my arm a squeeze.

"It all gets close and personal at some point." Eva would know.

"Is he a good kisser?" Gina asks. I bark out a shocked laugh. I knew it was coming, but I'm still surprised. It breaks the tension, though. Classic Gina move.

"Despite what Gina says, you're allowed a personal life," Denise says. "And it was kind of him to warn you. He cares about you." That question I keep ignoring swirls around in my head. I can't look at it now, though. We have work to do.

We spend the next several hours planning how to become invisible parts of Clare Leeman's life. Being a housekeeper will put Eva directly in Clare's world—where Clare lives and among her personal items. No one can perfectly hide their secrets all the time. Even the best officers and agents slip up.

We all agree that one of the hardest people to hide a secret from is a child. It's so easy to assume children aren't paying attention when, in fact, they are carefully taking in everything and remembering the smallest details with surprising accuracy. Becoming an activated terrorist is a big change. I doubt Clare has hidden such a change from her daughter, no matter how little time they've spent together. Having Denise drive her between daycare and preschool every day will provide us a good chance to see.

Although it's all in the file, I take some time to tell Gina about the Afghani assets and their case officers we'll be working with. I know them and worked with the case officers during one of my assignments in Afghanistan. They're excellent officers and treat their assets well. These foreign assets, including the one John met with, have been working with the CIA for several years, and the intel they've given us has been high value. But as the Agency recently learned, assets can be turned, especially if their loved ones are threatened.

"So, they want you in disguise when trailing Clare. Do you think you'll have surveillance to deal with?" Eva asks. I've been wondering the same thing.

"With Clare being activated, we need to plan for everything. One of my biggest concerns, though, is bumping into someone I know while tailing her. I've lived and worked in this area my whole life, so the chances of that happening a few times are pretty high. If she's as well trained as I believe she is, the second time she notices me won't be a coincidence to her."

"I think ya should get with Jake. Of all the tech guys, he's the best with disguise," Gina says.

"I agree. And I'm gonna need a brush-up on street disguise. The type I've been wearing the past few years has involved burkas."

"Yeah, that'll help you blend," Gina says as the rest of us laugh. We discuss a few more details and plan to meet first thing in the morning. I can tell they're excited to get to work —to do what they've been hired and trained to do. I'm still trying to process it all, though. The Agency has trained us to take in and process shocking situations quickly, but to have it involve John's ex-wife is crazy. I haven't had a cover since Nahla, so maybe I'm just rusty. Or maybe I can't do this anymore. That unsettling question I've been avoiding flutters to life in my mind.

I decline leftover chile rellenos and wish the team a good evening. I need to talk to John and I don't know how long that will take. And I need to wrap my head around all of this, which will require some alone time. I'm heading down the hall toward my cubicle when I see John. It looks like he's been waiting for me.

# 30

John guides me two doors down to an empty debriefing room. It's simple—a small table against the wall with two chairs pushed under it. The blinds are closed in the two windows and there are no active cameras. It's completely private.

I head toward a chair, but before I grab it, John pulls it out for me. I stop and stare at it. John is right next to me. I hear him breathing and smell his cologne. The chair is ready, waiting for me to sit down.

It's a personal gesture, pulling the chair out for me. The gesture belongs to John and Kate, not Officer Leeman and Officer Ross. Though many other men have pulled chairs out for me, this is different. The clutter in my mind drops off, like items on an overfilled shelf. The only item that remains is the question I keep avoiding.

I sit down and wrap my arms around my files, hugging them to my chest. John pulls the second chair out and sits facing me. Our knees bump. He puts his files on the desk, then gently takes mine from my arms and puts them on top of his. The pumpkin latte swirls in my stomach. I straighten my back and try not to look at my files.

"I have to ask you a question," I say.

"I'll tell you everything I'm allowed to tell you. And it's pretty obvious I'll push that rule to the limit." Neither of us laugh, though his eyes look a little less saggy.

"Did you ask me . . .," I pause. It's clear in my mind, but putting words to this question is awkward. "Did you begin a friendship with me because you want me and my team to take on this assignment?" It's not really how I want to say it, but it's out and by the look on John's face he understands the full weight of what I asked—are we being manipulated?

"No." He looks at my eyes for a few seconds. His effort to find words is obvious. They'll be direct, so I swallow and wait.

"I asked you to eat with me because I like you so much, I wanted to share a meal with you. I asked you to my home to meet my family because being with you feels safe and I wanted to share something precious with you. And I kissed you Sunday night because I couldn't help myself."

I believe him. His expression pleads for some sign that what he's done isn't a mistake. His arm is resting on the table and I reach over and touch it. He looks at my hand for a second and exhales through his mouth. "I had to know. Trust is kind of a thing with me," I say.

"I can understand that. Being tricked by your spouse can ruin you on trust. But I refuse to let that happen to me. I'm still able to recognize good in someone and I see good in you." A part of my heart stings as if blood is flowing to it for the first time in a long, long time.

Would he still feel this way, though, if he knew all I've done? If he knew about Nahla, about my crazy room? My eyes burn and before I can stop it, a tear slides down my cheek. John reaches in the chest pocket of his suit coat.

"Here," he says as he hands me a cloth handkerchief. I take it and laugh.

"Neal uses these." I wipe my cheek, leaving a smudge of makeup with the moisture.

"Really? My mom tells me to never leave the house without one."

"I like your mom."

"Well, she really likes you. And so does Livvy. In fact, we would all love for you to come to dinner again, soon." Was it just a few days ago that I sat in Rose's garden coloring with Livvy?

"How is this going to work? I like you, too. A lot. But how do we do the Agency and an operation involving your ex-wife? And us?" There. I said it. John slowly smiles at me.

"Very carefully. I know the CIA doesn't want their officers to have personal relationships, but it happens. So, we keep it personal, for now. And wouldn't it make this assignment, and any assignment, a little easier knowing someone you care about and who cares about you *really* knows what you do for a living?"

"Yes, it would."

"Although I don't think there's keeping anything from your team." We both laugh at the truth of this statement.

"They can sniff out anything."

"And that's why we want U-Tap on this assignment."

"Shouldn't you just take Livvy away?" I know the answer, but I have to ask it.

"You know, the slightest change could tip Clare off. If she suspects I'm on to her, she could take Livvy and disappear. And I assure you, Clare knows how to disappear. I'd never see my daughter again." His dark eyes grow darker and his jaw clenches. "As a father, I want to take my daughter and run. But as an officer, I need to find out the truth about Clare, to protect us all. So, as far as Livvy is concerned, everything needs to stay the same."

"Then it will stay the same." I bump his knee with mine. "We'll keep Livvy safe. Now let's see how my team and I can help you." I smile and slide my files off the stack. We have a lot of work to do and not much time to do it.

# 31

I'm standing in the attic of the house across from Clare's. It's a beautiful attic area. Empty, with pale-yellow walls, hardwood flooring and five-inch white molding. And a large window facing Clare's home. It would make a lovely office or bedroom, but so far is unused by the owners. Despite its beauty, it smells of dust and the strange combination of meals cooked weeks ago.

The two-story colonial is owned by a couple who won a three-week European cruise in a contest they forgot they entered sponsored by a vacation rental company. It was a deal no one could pass up—the couple rents their home for three weeks in exchange for a ton of money and the cruise of a lifetime. They'll never know a meshing of the FBI and the CIA will occupy their house in order to watch their neighbor who is believed to be a terrorist.

I look across at Clare's home. It's perfect. Every home on the street is perfect. There's not a blade of grass out of place. Do any children live in this neighborhood? If they do, where are the toys and bikes and chalk drawings on the sidewalks?

A Restoration Hardware catalog shows more life than this street in Bethesda. When they were married, Clare and John lived in the house John lives in now. I'm looking at the home Clare chose on her own, which tells us a little more about Clare Leeman—she likes her life to look catalog-perfect.

The last ten days have been an around-the-clock frenzy to get everyone operational. Clare's supposed business travels end today—Labor Day—so she'll take over Livvy's care full-time for a month to make up for lost time together over the summer.

This will be a big change for Livvy: full time with a mom she hasn't seen for months, full-time daycare and starting preschool. John and Rose are concerned with how Livvy will handle it all. But since John has always encouraged Clare to spend time with Livvy and has never caused problems with their joint custody arrangements, it would look unusual for him to do so now.

It all starts tomorrow, along with our efforts to discover Clare's plans. We've learned little about Clare. Her life appears to be squeaky-clean and impenetrable despite Gina's best efforts.

John and I have worked closely together at headquarters, but always with others around. There's been no personal time beyond a few exchanged words and a quick secret brush of hands. I daydream of having a normal dating relationship with John—to go to the movies and out to dinner instead of planning surveillance runs on his ex-wife.

But tonight will be a break from all that. I'm invited to John's for a Labor Day dinner with Rose and Livvy. What we'll really be celebrating is Livvy's start of preschool and daycare tomorrow and, hopefully, ease moving to the unwelcoming house I'm looking at. I ball my hands into a fist.

What a stark change from playing with neighborhood friends and lunch with Grandma every day to daycare and this sterile street. I look once more down both directions. The only thing missing is a Stepford Wife.

I won't be anywhere near this surveillance house once Livvy comes to Clare's tomorrow morning. This house has an outer building conveniently situated feet from the back alley with a covered walkway to the house. With the help of a few garden projects, agents, officers and technicians can come and go undetected. Still, we can't take the chance of Livvy seeing me. I relax my fists as I turn my back to the window. At least I have this evening with her, John and Rose.

## 32

John and I work in comfortable rhythm. I scrape the dishes and he rinses and loads them in the dishwasher. Having been pampered once with no clean-up duties, I demanded to take my turn. Of course, John helps me.

Livvy chose our menu for the evening, it being her special preschool celebration. The evening started out warm, so we dined inside, enjoying macaroni and cheese, sliced tomatoes from Rose's garden, and a beautiful green salad, also from the garden. Rose outdid herself again, the macaroni and cheese she made from scratch with three different types of cheese I can't pronounce. It was delectable.

I brought Livvy another gift. Starting preschool is a big thing, at least that's what I told myself when I picked out the Paw Patrol pencil bag filled with twenty-five pink pencils with cute interchangeable erasers. I don't know how well Paw Patrol will go over at Jarsdel, but Livvy loves it and that's all that matters. John and I watch her chatter to Rose about how important having all these pencils will be. Rose is giving

Livvy what appears to be sufficient oohs and ahhs. I smile, hoping neither forget this moment.

"She loves it," John whispers.

"I think so." It was between the pencils and pink hair bows. From what I see, I made the right choice. I wore a pale pink-silk blouse with my jeans because I've learned that pink is Livvy's favorite color. And my hair down because John has told me several times how much he likes it down and loose. Rose looks radiant in a white linen jumpsuit. John looks like he came from headquarters but with sleeves rolled up and no tie. He really looks like a model fresh from a photo shoot, and I'm working hard not to stare.

"Thank you," he adds. He brushes his hand across my lower back as he passes me to get more dirty dishes. I close my eyes for a second and steady my weight on both feet. Livvy and Rose are talking and neither notice anything.

We won't display affection in front of Livvy for a few reasons. One, our relationship is young and not to the point of including a child's hopes. And two, the last thing we need is for Livvy to go to Clare's tomorrow with stories about how much daddy likes his new girlfriend. To Livvy, I'm Kate-with-the-pretty-eyes, a nice lady from work who comes over sometimes and brings cool gifts. And it needs to stay that way for now.

For the past ten days at work, John and I have done a good job of holding up the protective barriers that hide our feelings for each other. Besides my team who can know from a glance what's going on, no one we work with suspects John and I care for each other. It's been tense. There have been many times we've needed to focus and haven't. It's so much nicer to watch John's lips as he talks rather than listen to what he's saying. And even nicer to watch him looking at my lips.

But now we're here, in the safety of John's home. Rose has reminded Livvy several times that bedtime will be earlier tonight, pointing out that preschool girls have to get their rest. But Rose smiles at John and me when she says this. She also mentioned more than once that she has a new book she can't wait to read. I asked her for the title, thinking I'd recommend it to Eva. When she scrambled for the title, I realized she was discretely assuring us we'd have some long-awaited private time.

Livvy and Rose come into the now-clean kitchen, Rose carrying a platter covered with cupcakes decorated with pink icing and an abundance of sprinkles. Rose baked them and Livvy decorated them. My assignment was ice cream, a task at which I am an expert. I brought vanilla swirled with sprinkles, a perfect match for the cupcakes. I also brought blackberry white chocolate, mint chocolate chip and, of course, rocky road.

You don't work around-the-clock with someone without picking up a few fun facts about each other. I now know that John loves white chocolate and can recite the new Paw Patrol movie by heart. And he knows how much I hate to run, but that I do it faithfully so I can have ice cream every night.

A not-so-fun-fact is that apparently, I now talk in my sleep. I fell asleep at my desk late one night. John let me sleep for a while but woke me up when I was saying things in Arabic about men he'd never heard of. He repeated the names back to me, but I brushed it off as stress and lack of sleep. What I didn't tell him was that the names were all insurgents I suspected discovered Nahla as an asset. Some barriers have to stay up for now.

Livvy is sitting on my lap, sharing my rocky road and cupcake, having gobbled up hers in record time. I'm playing a game, feeding her a bite and then letting her feed me a bite. Rose laughs and picks up the empty water pitcher and heads to the kitchen.

"I'm going to help you, Grandma." Livvy hands me the spoon and hops off my lap. John's sitting next to me and I follow his gaze as he watches Rose and Livvy move out of eyeshot.

He takes the spoon from my hand and smooths the back of it across my lips, leaving a smudge of melted ice cream. And then he leans over and quickly kisses it off. My head spins at his daring and the sudden warmth of his lips. When he pulls away, his eyes lock on mine. If you could kiss with a look, then that's what our eyes are doing. Over and over and over.

"Miss Kate, here's a napkin. You have ice cream on your mouth." I jump and bump Livvy's hand that's holding a paper napkin. "Daddy, are you teaching Miss Kate more manners?" I look back at John with a "did we just get caught?" look. He gives me a slight head shake.

"I am. She's got a lot of work to do," John answers. I try to make light of it with a chuckle, but Livvy looks disgusted with me.

"You have to have manners to go to preschool." She climbs back on my lap, telling me word-for-word the preschool rules she must follow. I remember reading them when going over Jarsdel's paperwork with Denise.

Rose places a full water pitcher on the table and gives her granddaughter a patient smile. "Five more minutes and then it's bedtime," she says. Livvy whines but stops herself and nods.

"Preschool girls have to get their sleep," Livvy says.

"How about you get your pjs on and pick a story out and I'll read it to you? Deal?" I ask. John smiles and kisses me a few times with his eyes.

"Deal!" Livvy slides off my lap, takes the waiting hand of her grandmother, and heads off to her bedroom. John and I watch as they go down the hall and out of sight. Our heads come together and our lips just touch when John's phone rings. He pauses for a second, his lips resting on mine as the phone announces the caller in its computerized voice: "Clare Leeman."

John waits to answer the phone until he's in the
kitchen. While walking there, his phone announces
Clare's name once more. I hunch forward and fold
my arms. When you're on assignment and required
to learn as much as you can about a person without meeting
them, it's easy to forget that they walk and talk and do
everyday things—like confirm a child exchange with her ex-
husband, which is what it sounds like is happening.

John is pleasant and upbeat. He has to be. Everything
needs to stay the same. But he was just kissing me. And now
with those same lips, he's pretending to be nice to his ex-wife
the terrorist. I force my shoulders back and exhale.

Rose appears from the hallway. "She's all yours." The
smile on her face slowly fades as she registers the conversation taking place in the kitchen. I stand up as Rose comes
toward me. "I'll say goodnight now. Thank you for coming."

"I wouldn't have missed it." Rose pulls me into an
embrace and holds me.

"Bless you for what you and your team are doing. I'll be

praying constantly for you," she whispers in my ear. Relief washes through me. She pulls away and takes both my hands. John told me his mother is one he trusts. Of course he would share this assignment with her. We give each other a knowing look as she squeezes my hands.

"I'm ready. I have a story. Are you coming?" comes Livvy's voice from her room. Rose and I smile and laugh, but I don't respond. I don't want to take the chance for Clare to hear my voice. I worried about coming over here tonight. What if Clare just shows up? But thankfully, surprise visits aren't a part of the joint custody agreement.

"Thank you," I whisper. Rose nods and then heads toward the sliding glass door and her cottage outback.

Livvy is in her bed, tucked under Paw Patrol blankets and sheets, wearing Paw Patrol pajamas, flanked by two Paw Patrol stuffed animals. In a chair against the wall is an opened suitcase revealing stacks of clothes. My stomach tightens at the change it represents.

"I picked out some books," she says, looking a little sheepish. On her lap is a stack of storybooks. I count out loud the books and stop at ten. She giggles in that childlike way that makes adults stop whatever they're doing and smile.

"How about we pick out three and we'll save the rest for another time." I kneel beside her bed, but she moves one of the stuffed toys and slides over a little.

"Lay by me and read," she demands. So, I slip off my sandals and lie down on her right side. She picks out the three largest, and I'm assuming longest, books and sets the rest on her left side. Her hair smells of shampoo and I catch whiffs of toothpaste from her freshly brushed teeth. She hands me one of the three and settles into my side. Her warmth and trust make me close my eyes for a second and inhale. "Start with this one," she says, pushing onto my lap a book with crayons on the cover.

I'm on page five, both of us laughing when John walks in. I keep reading while giving him a concerned look. He smiles and nods, telling me it's okay. Working closely with someone usually evolves into communicating with a look or slight motion. Spies take this form of communication to a heightened level. It comes easy for John and me.

He sets the rejected books on the floor and lies next to Livvy. She's so engrossed in the story she hardly notices but my heart quickens. I stumble over words and skip lines. John's chuckling, but I don't think it's because of the story. He's lying on his side, resting his head on his right hand. He scoots up a little and reaches his hand behind Livvy's head and runs a strand of my hair between his fingers. And I drop the book off the edge of the bed.

"You dropped the book. Oh, hi Daddy." This seems to have snapped Livvy out of her story trance.

"Hi sweetheart," he answers while I pick the book up and find the page. "Can I have a turn reading?" Livvy nods and I hand the book to John along with a "that wasn't fair" look. He laughs while Livvy tells him exactly where we were. He reads three pages, giving me a chance to watch Livvy and sneak glances at John's lips.

On the last page, Livvy's head is bobbing forward and her eyes are closed. John sets the book on the floor while I gently lean Livvy back on her pillow. I kiss her forehead and breathe in her little-girl smell. In unison, we carefully get up off the bed. John leans over and kisses her on the same spot while I quickly slip my sandals back on.

At the doorway, John turns the lights off and I notice a

Paw Patrol nightlight plugged in across her room, giving a warm, comforting glow. We walk out into the hallway and John pulls the door, leaving it open a few inches. He takes my hand and silently leads me down the hall, through the living room, and out the sliding glass door into the balmy evening air.

---

## 34

I t's not fully dark and the lights edging the garden path look iridescent in the dusk. All the blinds are closed in Rose's cottage, but there are lights on. I hope she really is enjoying a good book. I hear children playing and a car go past. We walk to the far corner of the yard where there's a fountain made of several levels of stone.

"I forgot you had a fountain," I say.

"We didn't have it on when you were here before. I'll show you why." He reaches to the side of it and flips a switch. The water churns and flows. As it hits the stone ledges, the sound increases until it's difficult to hear anything else. John leans down and puts his mouth against my ear. "Sometimes I need to talk to my mom."

And I understand. The two best ways to mask a conversation are loud machinery and moving water. John has created a beautiful way to have a safe conversation. He takes my face in his hands and puts his mouth back to my ear.

"Why are we spies?" I shake my head against his hands,

wondering where he's going with this question. "Because I want to kiss you whenever I want." And then he kisses me, deeply and for a long time. I've been kissed before, but nothing like this. I give myself up to it, pushing away the thought that it will end. When we do finally pull apart, we're breathless and smiling. He rests his forehead against mine and closes his eyes. I feel his breath on my face and I want to stay here, in this space where there aren't any barriers or secrets to keep—there's just us.

John takes my hand and leads me over to a cushioned love seat a few feet away from the fountain. It appears he calculated this spot so the fountain would mask voices, but the people talking could still hear each other.

We sit and John pulls me into his arms. His hands are firm against my back and his kiss is hungry, as if he's making up for the times he wanted to kiss me and couldn't. His desire for me is heady, dreamlike. *Why are we spies?* His question flashes through my mind and I blink.

His lips move to my ear and down my jaw as I fill my lungs with air. He leans up and kisses my forehead.

"I'll be right back." I watch him walk into the kitchen, then back with a glass of ice water. The water feels cool on my throat. He takes a sip and sets it on the grass. It's dark now, but I can still see his face by the walkway lights. His arms pull my head into his shoulder and the steady beat of his heart joins the tumble of water.

"Are you going to be okay tomorrow?" he asks. I move my head up and down, my cheek rubbing against the stiffness of his shirt. He smells of faded cologne and ice cream.

"You won't be alone out there."

"No, I won't. Gina and her tech guys have me taken care of." I'll have a state-of-the-art earpiece that will keep me

ted t Jhn and my team. "Dn't wrry abut me. I've
dne this lts f times."

"But it's been a while since yu've been in disguise here,
in a familiar city." He's right. The familiar can make it easy t
relax when yu're in disguise, trying t keep up a cmpletely
different prfile. There's nthing like a war-trn village in
the Middle East t keep yu n yur tes. "I just want yu
safe." I wrap my arms arund his waist and give him a
squeeze befre I pull away t see his face.

"D yu really think she's a terrrist?" I have t ask this
questin smetime tnight. He lks at me fr a few secnds
and then turns his gaze t the huse.

"I d."

"And yu never suspected her? Never questined sme-
thing dd she did?" He lks back t me and puts a strand f
my hair behind my ear.

"She was my wife. I wasn't lking fr anything, least f
all her being a terrrist. I trusted her." Trust. He has a pint.
Why wuld anyne suspect their spuse f being a terrrist?
I might, thugh. *Why are we spies?* Wuld I have such a
prblem with trust if I weren't a spy?

"Can I ask why yu divrced?" Anther hard questin I
need t ask.

"Kate, yu can ask me anything." He kisses me sftly,
then takes my hand and weaves his fingers thrugh mine.
"Yu knw the scripture Neal uses t teach everyne abut
truth and trust? 'By their fruits yea shall knw them.'" I nd.
"Well, when Clare and I married, I thught I knew her by
the 'fruits' f her life. But then they changed. What she
brught abut in her life became different." He lets g f my
hand and picks up the glass f water. He takes a few sips and
ffers it t me, but I shake my head. He hlds the glass in

both hands and rubs the rim with his thumb. I want him to keep talking.

"Different how?"

"It was hard to pin-point at first. Everything I noticed sounded nit-picky. But looking back, I see the controlling patterns of a sociopath, especially after Livvy was born. We quit talking and grew apart. I loved her, or I thought I did. The disconnect didn't hurt her like it did me, though. It just made her mad. But did I suspect her of being a terrorist? No. That's why I had to go to Afghanistan and talk to the asset. I didn't learn anything new, but I had to hear it in person."

I get that. Yet, it's hard to hear a man you care about talk of another woman he once loved. In a weird, selfish way it helps if that other woman is a sociopathic terrorist. I push this thought aside.

"So, the first clue was learning of her possible activation?" This is what he's told the CIA, but I ask it anyway.

"Yeah. But hindsight is so clear. I keep telling myself I didn't see any signs because I wasn't looking. If I had been looking, though, would I have seen someone who's been radicalized? Maybe. But I don't think so. I was tricked."

"I'm so sorry," I say. He grins and then kisses me again.

"I won't let it change me. I can't. What kind of life would I have if I couldn't trust?" The back of my throat tightens. I take the glass from his hand and swallow the last of the water, then set it down.

"Not a very good one," I answer. I choke on the last word and clear my throat.

"I was really messed up after the divorce. I prayed constantly that I'd meet someone I could trust, that I could feel what it is to trust again. I just didn't think it would be while figuring out my ex-wife, the terrorist." We both look at each other, the reality of what he just said registering, and I can tell he's trying not to laugh.

"You'd think you could come up with a better line than that," I say. We bust out laughing and it takes us a minute to gain control. Is it just spies who would think this is funny?

"I guess I'm not very smooth," he says, still laughing.

I lean up and put my lips on his so he can feel mine move when I talk. "I don't care about smooth. I care about being honest." This kiss leaves all the rest in the dust. He pulls away first.

"I want to build our relationship on trust and respect," he says. He takes a second to breathe through his nose. "But we lie for a living. We deceive and manipulate while convincing everyone around us we're telling the truth. And we break laws. Oh man, the laws we are breaking just on this assignment would put any of us away for life."

"You're right." *Why are we spies?* "But we don't have to lie to each other." He holds my eyes with his and runs his thumb across my cheekbone.

"Kate, there are things about this assignment I can't tell you right now. I'm having to ask for your trust before I've earned it. Can you do that?"

*You can trust him,* says the voice in my head. Can I? And can I trust myself? I still have so many questions. And there are things I haven't shared with him, like what really happened to Nahla. And my crazy room. I wrap my arms around his shoulders and rest my head next to his. "I can, but I'm afraid."

He turns his head and kisses my ear, my cheek, and all along my jaw until he reaches my lips. I slow his kiss down, taking my time, knowing I must leave soon. We could both go a long time without sleep and be sharp, but it would be good if we faced tomorrow rested. There's a lot at stake.

"I want to stay in this safe place, next to you and the fountain where we can say whatever we want," I say. He gives me a slow smile.

"And where we can kiss whenever we want," he says. I smile back, but not with my eyes. *Why are we spies?* The price of being a spy seems painfully high right now. I kiss him one more time and then get up to leave.

## 35

I shouldn't be here in the attic, watching Clare's house. I'm supposed to be waiting in a car a block over so I can follow her to work, or wherever she's going this morning. But I wanted to see John and Clare together. Despite who and what Clare is, it will hurt to see her beside him. Like ripping a Band-Aid off. But I want to do the ripping.

Everything is ready for the first day of surveillance. We scheduled the cleaning crew from Appearance Maid Service for midday service, and Denise is lined up to drive Livvy with a group of daycare children to their first day at Jarsdel Preschool. Gina and a team of tech guys will continue their attempts at hacking into Clare's cyber life, which so far is tied up as perfectly as her home. It's driving Gina crazy. My last conversation with her was at three this morning. She was so wired on Red Bull and talking so fast I could hardly understand her.

"Who is this woman?" Gina yelled into the phone. At first, I thought I had overslept. But when I saw what time it was, it registered what was going on. Gina has been working nonstop to find a way into Clare's life and she's taking the failure personal. It's a good thing she sent her daughters to visit her mom in Georgia.

"Well, we're pretty sure she's a terrorist," I answered, groggy from sleep.

"I can't even hack her freakin' Netflix account!" She gave me a lengthy list of all her hacking accomplishments, some of which were new to me. I tried to assure her and told her to get a few hours of sleep before morning.

I see movement on the street. It's the FBI agents posing as the retired couple renting this home. They're returning from their morning walk. I can see their lips—they'll shower and eat breakfast and then head out for a day of sightseeing in our nation's capital. They're maintaining their covers perfectly.

Garbage trucks and service vans, carefully scheduled to move along the back alley, bring in people and supplies unnoticed. I came to the house this morning in a city gas service van, along with two FBI agents who kept staring at my legs. I'm wearing a black skirt with a beige blouse and a pair of extremely uncomfortable leggings that look like "support hose for my meaty calves," as Jake put it. The varicose veins were an added touch. Since I am an officer-in-charge, the FBI agents were trying not to laugh. But they weren't trying that hard.

Today I'm a sixty-something legal secretary. Thanks to a graying wig, some facial prosthesis under a brilliant makeup job, and overall body padding, I have the look of a tired, overworked, overweight woman. Disguise only goes one way —older, larger, taller. It's impossible to go the other way.

My car title and my pocket litter—all the normal,

everyday items a woman would carry in her purse—identi-
fies me as Margaret Neil. And I'm wearing my old friends,
the contact lenses, to give me brown eyes.

I don't care how unattractive and uncomfortable I may
look and feel, this disguise is a protection from being identi-
fied. I could sit across from Manny and he wouldn't recognize me. Denise reminded me of this last night. She called
me right before I went to bed.

"It's your body armor. Remember that out there," she
said, referring to Jake's disguise.

"Crazy that varicose veins can be right up there with a
Kevlar vest."

"Crazy, but true. Except you're not hiding behind those
bulging blue veins, you're becoming them. Be your profile
and you'll be safe. You'll be invisible," she said. Warmth
filled my face. She's done disguise. She gets it.

"Be the veins. I am the veins. I'm one with the veins," I
recited, making her burst out laughing. I look down at my
fake veins, milky blue in the morning light from the window,
and smile. And then I look back out on the street.

I know from which direction John will come, but I still
check both ways. He's a little late. I hope Livvy's okay. John
texted me early this morning, while Jake was working on me,
and said Livvy had repacked her backpack five times
already.

Agents and officers come in and out of the attic. I don't
sense any competition among them, but, rather, an anxious
sense of purpose. Agent Maxwell catches my eye and gives
me a quick nod. I smile then turn my gaze on the street
below.

Finally, I see John's truck coming. It lines up with Clare's
front door and he has Livvy out on the sidewalk like a parent

that's late. My stomach turns over when I see Livvy's frowning face. She clutches her backpack to her chest and John carries the suitcase I saw in her room last night. She has a pink dress on and her hair falls in ringlets over her shoulders. He rings the doorbell and waits. My heart is pounding and I press my lips together to keep from gritting my teeth and causing the dental facade to pinch my gums.

The door swings open and I see a toothy smile, blonde hair, and a cream-colored dress that probably costs my monthly paycheck. And there they are together, what once was a family. John smiles and talks to her with the mouth I kissed last night. Clare responds and looks as perfect as her house and the street it's on. He was once so in love with her he wanted to spend the rest of his life with her. He trusted her and had a child with her. And she tricked him.

Livvy is clinging to John's leg and I remind myself it's been weeks since she's seen her mother. I want to blow this whole assignment, grab Livvy and take her back to the cozy street with the bikes and chalk drawings. But I can't. I just stand here watching as John peels Livvy from his leg and Clare squats, finally coaxing a reluctant hug from her daughter. And then I turn and go. I have two minutes to meet the gas van on its way back across the alley.

## 36

I'm driving a dark-gray Honda Accord and am parked down from the main exit of Clare's neighborhood with the engine off—no parking lights that would draw attention. I would think a mother who hasn't seen her daughter in weeks would want to spend a little time with her and not take her to daycare until it was absolutely necessary. Or maybe even take the morning off and take her daughter to preschool herself. But my gut tells me Clare will be by any minute.

I feel for the fake wedding ring, a wide gold band like my mother's, and press the bottom quickly, twice. This turns on the earpiece in my right ear. My communication device is undetectable to even the closest inspection, won't set off a bug sweeper, and will work anywhere like Jack Bauer's cell phone. A series of presses to the back connects me to John and my team.

I wait, pulling on the side of my eye because the contacts are bothering me. I try to adjust the leggings, but they're just going to be uncomfortable. I'm grateful, though, after the balmy evening last night, that this morning there's a touch of fall in the air. The humidity would be awful in this disguise. I've endured much worse, though, and mentally go through my profile one more time. I'm Margaret Neil. I work for Mirren and Mirren Law Firm. I'm married to Robert Neil and have lived in the DC area for twenty-three years.

I check my large black purse that holds my pocket clutter but gives me enough space to perform a quick-change. Underneath my clothes is a different outfit—a complete profile change I can do slyly, piece by piece, within thirty-seven—or fewer—perfectly choreographed steps. No one notices people adjusting their clothes in a crowd, especially if everyone is staring down at their phones. While I'm following Clare, I'll always have a quick-change with me. Another layer of body armor.

I've practiced various quick-changes over and over while walking the hallway of headquarters. When he could, John would walk with me and count out the steps. Under Jake's masterful eye, I learned subtle changes that could make the difference between being noticed or staying invisible. I swallow and count it out again, visualizing each disguise change with each step.

A silver BMW passes. It's Clare, right on time with Livvy in the back seat. I know the way to Nethercott and let two more cars pass by before pulling out. Clare takes the direct route. No side trips to the park for a half hour of play or quick stop for a hot cocoa with whip cream and sprinkles to mark the beginning of preschool later today.

There's a doctor's office next to Nethercott and I pull in and park. I can see Clare's car but don't have a clear visual of Livvy. The door to the daycare opens and closes, and I imagine them going through the check-in procedure. It's been weeks since Livvy has been there, which can feel like a lifetime to a four-year-old. For the second time this morning, I want to blow the top off this whole thing, grab Livvy, and spend the day coloring with her in Rose's garden.

In what seems like barely enough time to sign a few forms and kiss the top of Livvy's head, Clare is back out to her car. The route to Clare's office building is a five-minute stretch of surface streets followed by a good thirty minutes on the freeway, or longer depending on the traffic. This time of morning it's usually awful. I settle in for what could be a long commute. I hear a click in my ear.

"Kate, you there?" John's voice sounds urgent.

"I'm here. Everything okay?"

"Yeah. I'm on my way into headquarters. The tech guys called and said they were having problems getting through on your earpiece. Has Clare left yet?"

"She has. We're just pulling onto the freeway. Looks like we'll be here for a bit. And the earpiece is working fine. I just turned it off for a while. I was at the house and saw you bring Livvy." There's a pause—three breaths for both of us.

John sighs. "I would have done the same thing."

"You doing okay?" I ask. I'm at a complete stop in traffic, one lane over and three cars behind Clare. She's talking on the phone and I wish I were ahead of her so I could read her lips, though looking in your rearview mirror for any length of time can be a dead giveaway—a surveillance rookie-move.

"Not really. I had to peel Livvy off of me and force her to go to Clare, though you probably saw all that."

"I did. I can't imagine a worse feeling, especially with what we suspect about Clare. I wanted to chuck this whole assignment, grab Livvy, and run."

"Me, too. Thanks for saying that, and for being with me.

This would be really hard to do without you." Traffic moves a little and then stops again. It looks like it will be this way for miles. "If I were with you, I'd kiss you no matter what anyone thinks."

"You wouldn't recognize me."

"Oh, I don't know about that. Jake sent Neal and me a picture of you this morning. He's pretty proud of his work."

I laugh but keep my body language as a bored driver—I don't want any sudden movements to draw the attention of other drivers.

"I don't know about the calves, but I'd know those lips anywhere. I can still feel them." My heart pushes against my chest and I roll my lips in, remembering his last kiss.

"I wish I would have kissed you one more time."

"Okay. Y'all probably should've kissed a lot longer," Gina says. I grab the steering wheel and rear back in my seat. So much for masking body language.

"Gina?" I blurt while John laughs.

"Hi, Gina," he says and laughs some more.

"Hi, you handsome Bondman. Sorry to interrupt, but I need to make sure Kate's earpiece is working right. My computer shows it wasn't on this morning. It's obviously on now, though."

"Yeah, it's on now. I didn't hear a click when you came on," I say. Can there be a little privacy on this device?

"I heard it click," John says. "Right before . . . that last thing you said."

"It clicked, Kate. You were just thinkin' about your regrets. Well, as much as I'd like to hang out with y'all, I've got a terrorist to hack. John, I just made a picture of Kate in today's getup as your screensaver so you'll have that to enjoy when you're missin' her today. Kate, honey, don't you worry.

There's no way you'll have those calves when you're my age. Now, you two get back to that conversation about lips. Talk to ya later." There's a click and Gina's gone.

"I guess I'm gonna have to listen for those clicks," I say to John's quiet chuckling.

"Yeah. But it's okay. Do you know how good it feels to hear you say you want to kiss me? And I didn't think I could feel good about anything today." I grin and lighten my grip on the steering wheel.

"Traffic is moving. I'll let you know when Clare gets to work," and we say goodbye, which is good because, despite all my training, trying to maneuver traffic while talking to John about kissing would be hard. And I need to get my head back in my profile. I'll be on the street with Clare in a few minutes.

## 37

I 'm walking ten paces behind Clare. Her gait is quick and purposeful, surprisingly so in the expensive navy stilettos she's wearing. She looks like the type that spends a good portion of each day in shoes like those and could probably run a mile in them and not teeter once.

I can smell her perfume. It's the pungent, chemical-like fragrance that dominates a room and forces shallow breathing in an elevator. Did she wear it when she was married to John? Does he like that kind of perfume?

I drop back a few paces, forcing those questions from my mind. Whether or not we recognize it, what we feel sends a powerful message to those around us. One of the worst things a spy can do is give into fear. Jealousy would have to come in at a close second. I'm a tired legal secretary, trudging my way to another day at work, not the jealous girlfriend of Clare's ex-husband. And if Clare is who we think she is, she'll pick up on the slightest nuances around her.

The entire front of Harrod and Raynott Financial is glass. Even after years of surveillance, I still fight the urge to look through the glass as she walks in the front door. But a spy can't ever look back. Looking back is letting the person you are surveilling—or the person surveilling you—know you know they're there. It's a dead giveaway. Regardless of the side you're on, you can't let them know you know what they're up to because then the game is up and people run.

My gaze stays downcast and my walk slow and heavy. I continue past her building and around the block, beginning a well-planned circuitous pattern of foot surveillance broken up by stops in coffee shops, stores, and a café for lunch. I'll sip my coffee and scroll on my fake phone. A wireless device can be used against me as a tracker, so Jake made me a shell of a phone with images and text on it so it would look like I'm scrolling through text messages, social media, or reading a book.

It's a long day. I'd almost forgotten how boring surveillance can be. John checked on me, regularly, but he needed to be brief, just giving me updates. I could pretend to be talking on a wireless but that would require me to have a device in my ear, altering the sounds around me and I won't do that. And I don't want anyone overhearing even the most cryptic exchanges with John or my team.

Clare sticks to her normal schedule, leaving work a little after five and driving straight to pick up Livvy. Denise reported that Livvy seemed nervous about going to preschool, but on the drive back to daycare appeared happy, talking with the other children about a playdate coming up. This is the best news I've had all day. Even better than the lip conversation with John.

Eva said Clare's house was a pillar of perfection. Eva hid a bug detector in her duster, but there was nothing. Still unable to find a chink in Clare's cyber armor, Gina swore when she learned this—and Gina never swears. The only thing that seemed out of place were Livvy's drawings, several of them, that covered Clare's refrigerator. It surprised me Clare would allow this, but couldn't keep from smiling, thinking of the drawings adorning my refrigerator at home.

Liberated from my disguise and fresh from a shower, I'm in leggings and a T-shirt lying on my floor, the ceiling fan directly above me. I have a pint of rocky road and a spoon next to me. I earned it from the miles of streets I walked today. It reminded me of my surveillance detection training on the streets of DC before they sent me on my first foreign assignment.

My laptop dings, letting me know that Eva and Denise are ready to give me some more details about their day. And I'm sure they've talked to Gina, so they will tease me about John too. I take my ice cream with me to the table where my laptop waits and click a few keys. Denise's and Eva's faces appear. They are a welcome sight after a long day of being someone else.

"I bet you're exhausted," Denise says. Her voice is soothing, as always.

"Yep. And I earned this," I answer as I take the lid off my pint and test its softness with the spoon. It's perfect and I scoop out a bite.

"It's nice to see you no longer think John's a horrible human being. At least not his lips," Eva says. I laugh through my bite and almost choke.

"He's very nice. It's hard to imagine him married to Clare." I can't help but put this out there. "Tell me what you think after today."

Despite her calm voice, Denise rubs her forehead and blinks more than normal. "I was at the Nithercott for Livvy's drop-off and pickup. My gut tells me she's afraid of her mom."

"That's what I think, too. I watched from the surveillance house as John dropped her off." They both raise their eyebrows but say nothing. "And I've been to John's home twice and have FaceTimed a lot, and Livvy never talks about her mom. That can't be normal."

"It's not normal," Denise says. "Unless you're afraid. Frightened children are usually silent children."

"I'll tell you what's not normal is that woman's house," Eva says. "No one is allowed to live in that house. It's definitely no home." I look at the breakfast dishes still in my sink and glance over at the load of unfolded laundry on my sofa. I live in my home. *Especially your crazy room,* says the voice in my head. I scowl at the comparison and push it from my thoughts.

"So, there's a bunch of drawings on the refrigerator?" I ask.

"Yeah. I counted eight. They covered the front of the fridge and freezer. But there was no other sign of a child in that house. None. No toys, blankets, books, or anything." I narrow my eyes. What a cold environment for Livvy. But why the drawings? I take another bite of ice cream.

"What were the drawings of?" I ask.

"I couldn't spend a lot of time looking at them. I'm new on the crew and the other cleaners were watching me. I caught some buildings and people. One thing I did notice is that each drawing was dated by an adult; I'm assuming Clare. They said 'playdate August eighth' for example. It seemed strange she would associate them with a playdate. When I saved my kids' drawings, I always put their age on the drawing."

"So did I," says Denise. "There was talk of another play-date this Saturday." We all give each other a familiar expression.

"I know with the FBI working with us, we can plant a bug in her home. But John and I are certain she sweeps it daily. If Clare knows she's being watched, she'll run. And she could take Livvy with her." They tighten their lips and shake their heads. "Gina will get into her world soon. Until then, we'll have to keep gathering all the human intel we can."

"So, who will you be tomorrow?" Denise asks. I smile, thinking of the many days she walked the streets of New York, each day as a different person.

"Another middle-aged secretary. But with thinner calves." We laugh as I scrape the bottom of my pint. I should probably run tomorrow evening, no matter how much I walk during the day. My phone rings and announces John's name.

"We'll let you go," Denise says.

"Tell John we said hi," Eva adds. I laugh and thank them and say goodbye. Their faces vanish with a click and I pick up my phone.

## 38

I can't stop yawning as I follow Clare and Livvy to Nithercott. I'll have no problem looking like a tired secretary today. John and I talked late last night—some about work, but mainly about other things. I think he sensed I needed to detox from my day, so he asked me silly stuff about my childhood. It didn't feel silly, though. It was a huge release. It would be so hard to have a boyfriend I had to hide my life from, like having another cover. Maybe that's why I haven't had a serious relationship since I began working for the Agency. *There are other reasons, too*, says the voice in my head. Before it can tell me more, I hear a click.

"I have a new screensaver this morning," John says. His voice warms my ear.

"You know, this gray-bob wig is growing on me."

"Jake did a great job on you this morning. I bribed Gina with a Red Bull if she'd keep the screensavers coming." Gina's hitting the hard stuff early.

"Why have we not been able to get inside Clare's world?" I ask it like the rhetorical question it's become.

"Because it's not just her. She's got a huge terrorist organization behind her. You know the money they have."

"That reminds me. You know what her clothes cost, right?"

"Yeah. The shoes she wore yesterday cost my paycheck. Just one more red flag. She started dressing like that after we divorced. I wonder if, once she was free from me, she didn't have to hide the extra money she was getting."

"Could be. It doesn't seem like she spends a lot of money on Livvy. Except for the most expensive daycare in the city that she just pulled into."

"Nethercott, and Jarsdel, are more about Clare than Livvy. I'd like to know how much money she used to buy her way in at the last minute." I park across the street and can see them going in. And Livvy is clutching her backpack like it's a security blanket.

"Why aren't we seeing anything from her? If she's really activated, why isn't she showing us something?" I hear John take a couple of deep breaths.

"I don't know. But until we do, we'll keep gathering intel," he says.

"Maybe she'll go to lunch with someone today and I can get close enough to read her lips." Having a conversation with a member of her cell at her work would be a significant risk. But safer to do in a busy restaurant.

"I wish you could come and read my lips for a few hours." I tap the steering wheel as I pull out onto the street, a few cars behind Clare. For a split second, I want to head my car toward headquarters.

"You really want to spend hours kissing a sixty-year-old secretary?" I say with a chuckle.

"I want to be with you. I don't care what you look like."

The back of my throat burns and I blink against the moisture flooding my contacts. I'm surprised by the emotion this simple declaration brings.

"Thank you for saying that."

"I better go. Gina keeps texting me. I don't know if the Red Bull was such a good idea. I'll check in with you in a few hours." I laugh as he clicks off.

The morning went the same as yesterday, right down to the awful traffic and Clare's hideous perfume. I'm about halfway through my second cup of coffee, in a Starbucks across the street from her building, when I see her come out the main entrance. She's wearing a red dress with leopard-print stilettos today, which makes my job easier. My heart races when I see her come toward the Starbucks. I breathe through my nose and then take another sip of coffee. *Just keep scrolling on your phone,* the voice in my head tells me.

The door opens and her perfume rolls in ahead of her. She walks past me to get in line, her dress brushing the empty chair to my left. Her voice is high pitched and demanding as she tells the barista what she wants. I take another sip of coffee and scroll my fake phone with my thumb. I've looked at the same images a hundred times in the last day and a half, but I bring my eyebrows together in concentration, as if what's on the screen has captivated my attention.

Clare sits two tables away from me. She takes a sip of her coffee that looks much more like a dessert and gets her phone out. I offer a quick prayer that she feels safely isolated and calls someone in her cell. I scrunch my eyebrows even more. Why would I pray now? She dials and starts talking. No need to read lips. Her voice is so distinct, it carries easily to me.

Her side of the conversation sounds work related. There are company names and money amounts. I shift in my chair and cross my legs. Someone sitting completely still is unnatural. We humans are constantly trying to be more comfortable. I take another sip of coffee and listen, but it's all work. She gets louder as she seems to convince someone to agree to an amount of money. She's not worried about anyone overhearing her. Disappointment sinks to the bottom of my coffee-filled stomach.

Clare ends the conversation and for a second, I think she may make another call, but she doesn't. Without using a mirror, she quickly applies some lip gloss, then picks up her half-empty coffee-dessert and walks out the door. I watch as she walks across the street and back into Harrod and Raynott. She doesn't notice anyone around her.

I've seen my share of terrorists. They take in everything around them, process it, file it away. Nothing goes unnoticed. What I just saw from Clare didn't feel like any of that. Maybe she's not a terrorist. Or maybe she's the best of the best. Either way, I got nothing from this encounter.

I get up to leave. I need to find a quiet spot to report this to John.

TODAY WAS A CARBON-COPY OF YESTERDAY. Other than the occasional visit to Starbucks, Clare does nothing out of the ordinary. The waiting is unbearable. Is she really a terrorist? And if she's activated, why has she not done anything? Our experience has been that when an activation phrase is given to a terrorist cell, things happen—fast. But all we see is Clare sticking to a regimented schedule.

We need to look over all our intel again. John set up a live video meeting with one of the three case officers in Afghanistan that claims Clare's been activated. I wasn't in on the first meeting with the three, so I'm looking forward to talking with Officer Sayed tonight. And I want to see John.

The sun is setting as I pull into headquarters. I drove with my window down, the cool air helping to dry my freshly washed hair. I didn't have much time but would not give up my shower. It was a long day of surveillance walks.

I park and take a minute to pull my hair into a messy bun. My normal work outfit—a navy skirt and white blouse —feels deliciously light compared to a disguise with quick-change pieces underneath.

I put my identification on and the pull of the cord on the back of my neck is at once familiar. It's been days since I've worn it. Switching from a disguise back to yourself is confusing. But the small touchstones of identity, like my CIA lanyard, are grounding.

Walking through the entrance, my partially dry scalp tingles in the cool air-conditioned foyer. My step is lighter with each familiar face I greet. Has it just been a few days since I've been here?

I turn the corner of a hallway and feel a hand brush against my arm. Adrenalin rushes up my neck and I miss a step. Strong hands steady me and then pull me through an open door.

## 39

"Come in here," John says in my ear. I'm dizzy as his scent mixes with the adrenalin rush. It's an empty office. I barely glimpse it and him before he turns the lights out. His warm hands line my face. "I know this is risky, but I just need a minute alone with you."

His lips find mine and he kisses me in one long, fluid motion. The room drops away. Everything. We could be standing on my front porch, in the park next to Manny's, or by his fountain—I wouldn't know. For a few moments, we drink each other up.

"We have to go," I say while taking a breath.

"I know." He kisses me once more and pulls me close to him. I melt into his chest. The thought of this hug has got me through miles following Clare on the sidewalks of this city. I grip his suit coat and bury my face in his neck.

"Tell me again that you trust me, no matter how this all turns out with Clare." Why can't I hear that word without my stomach twisting? *Because you have issues with it and you're hiding your crazy from this ridiculously handsome man,* says the voice in my head.

"I trust you, no matter what," I answer. My stomach twists even more. I *do* trust John. *But do you trust yourself?* Why is the voice in my head doing this to me?

We need to leave, but I pull his mouth down to mine. I'm hungry in my need to erase everything, especially the voice in my head with his lips. It works until a call comes in on his phone.

"John Leeman," he answers. I can't make out what the other person is saying over my breathing. "Okay. I have a few things to go over with Kate and then we'll be there," he says and ends the call. "They'll be ready in a few minutes."

"So, we need to go."

"Yeah. Neal's probably there already, waiting for us." This meeting will be the three of us. The fewer people knowing the identity of Officer Sayed and his whereabouts, the better.

John turns the light on and we both squint against the brightness. I want to stay in this moment with John, in the dark where we could be anywhere but Langley.

"I'm glad you found me." He winks and smiles like a model.

"Just lurking in the hallway, waiting to grab innocent women."

"Well, we *are* spies." We both laugh and I hug him one more time. It hurts to let him go.

"You go first," he says and opens the door. I slide out into a thankfully empty hallway. We could have both left the room together. We had some things to go over before our meeting, like John told the tech guy. But I think there's a feeling of getting away with something that separates us from work—at least for me there is.

The door to the conference room is open and Neal is waiting inside. To my surprise, Eva and Denise are waiting there. They both stand straight, leaning slightly forward. It's been a long day for both of them, but they're engaged and ready to work.

"We were invited to the party at the last minute," Eva says as they each give me a hug. I can still smell John's cologne on my blouse and wonder who else can.

"You doing okay?" Neal asks.

"Great," I say too loudly. I clear my throat. "No Gina?" I ask in a normal volume.

Neal's eyebrows come together. That's not good.

"She was planning on coming," Eva says, "but has been trying to test out a way to get into Clare's wireless. She and one of her tech guys are up in a bucket truck posing as cable workers repairing something on a pole."

"The poor tech guy is afraid of heights. But I think he's more afraid of Gina. She said something about not coming down until she's in. Poor guy looked petrified with fear," Denise says. I can't help but laugh at the image. I hope she laid off the Red Bull.

When John walks in, he looks at me and with his eyes does a repeat of what we just did in the empty office. And then he gives me a sheepish grin because he knows none of it was lost on the other three.

"John, I invited Eva and Denise," Neal says. "I think some information Officer Sayed has will directly affect their assignments. Let's get going. Sayed's been waiting." He gives John and me a quick glance, just long enough to let us know he knows full well what "things" we had to go over.

Neal taps a speaker in front of him. I was told this meeting would be a video feed and was looking forward to seeing Sayed's face, to make my own assessment on what he knows about Clare. But I'm sure the decision to change to audio was out of consideration for Eva and Denise. Keeping Sayed's full identity protected is as much a safeguard for them as it is for him—the less Eva and Denise know, the less of a target they are.

"Officer Sayed, you there?" Neal asks.

"I'm here," says a man's deep voice. I've met Sayed a few times when I was in Afghanistan, so I picture his image— tall, lithe, mid-thirties and of Arabic decent. He needs little by way of disguise, just a beard and clothing.

Neal introduces each of us. Sayed is polite to Eva and Denise, remembers me, and is comfortably familiar with John.

"Sayed, will you review with us how you and the other officers determined that Clare Leeman is a part of an acti- vated terrorist cell." I can tell Neal's going through formali- ties for Eva's and Denise's benefit.

Sayed tells us the info we already know, Clare's connec- tions with the high-ranking terrorists, money trails and references to the extensive amount of chatter regarding her cell's activation, and the timing of trips coinciding with training and meetings. Sayed goes through it all as if from memory. It doesn't sound like he's referring to any notes. He's been living this information for a while. I watch as John's face turns pale. This must be painful every time he hears it.

"So, you have additional information about her activa- tion?" John asks.

"Yes. We just found out that the activation phrase had something to do with 'coloring outside the lines.'" My eyes snap up and dart back and forth to everyone else's darting eyes.

"The only thing in Clare's home that seems unusual for her are drawings she's put on her refrigerator. They're by her daughter and other children she's played with. They're unusual because they're the only evidence Clare has that a child lives with her," Eva says.

"Have you seen these pictures? Is there anything peculiar about them?"

"Yes. They're dated weirdly. They have the word 'play-date' and the date on each."

There's a pause. I could almost hear the wheels churning in Sayed's head. "The only thing my wife would put on drawings was our child's name and age."

"Same here," says Eva. Denise and Neal agree.

"What were the drawings of?" Sayed asks.

"They didn't give me the kitchen to clean, so I only had quick glances as I'd walk through. But there were people and buildings. The dates were hard to miss because they were in bold lettering. It looked like Clare used a black Sharpie," Eva answered.

"The next cleaning is tomorrow," Neal says. "Eva, you need to make sure you clean the kitchen."

"I will," she says.

"You also need to get photos of those drawings. Have a tech guy hook you up with a camera," Neal adds.

"Got it," I say.

"There's something I heard the children say today that, considering all this, seems unusual," Denise says. "There's a scheduled playdate at Clare's house on Saturday. They seemed excited about it but were asking each other what they were supposed to draw, as if they had to come with specifically drawn pictures."

"Is this the first time they've said this?" I ask.

"Yes. I was just getting ready to call you when Neal invited us to this meeting." There's another long pause. "Could Clare be using the drawings to communicate with her cell?"

Neal and John look at each other—the eye-to-eye exchange two people have when something they hoped wouldn't happen, happens. That Clare could use Livvy as part of her cover has always been on the radar. But to have Livvy and her daycare playmates have an active role turns my stomach. And have John and Neal suspected this?

"It sounds like you need some solid intel and soon," Sayed says.

"We've got more questions than answers, that's for sure," John says.

"I've gotta go. But I'd appreciate being kept in the loop. I have a bad feeling about this one."

"So do we," I say. I look to John and then Neal and then back to John. What aren't they telling me?

John assures Sayed we'll keep in touch and disconnects the call. Eva and Denise get up to leave, giving me a quick goodbye before heading off to find the tech guy John suggested for Eva's hidden camera.

I should go too because I need to be back here early in the morning for another of Jake's transformations, but I hang back. I have a myriad of questions swirling in my head. Are other parents a part of Clare's cell? Who else is seeing these drawings? What exactly do they communicate? But there's only one question I know these two men can answer right now.

## 40

"Have you suspected all along that Clare could use Olivia like this? Forcing her to help communicate with others in her cell?" I ask Neal and John. They both stare at me for three long beats. The color drains from John's face again.

"Kate, you've been around terrorists enough to know they'll use anything to accomplish their mission," Neal says. "They'll strap a bomb onto a kid and send them into a crowd. But if we made Olivia the focus, it could blind us to what they're really up to, a strategy Clare and her cell could depend on." He's right. But this has become personal. Images of Nahla flash through my mind and I swallow.

John's eyes are round and pleading. Is this why he keeps asking me to trust him? So I won't make this assignment so personal that I mess up . . . again. I need rest and air. I need to get out of this building. And I need to talk with Gina.

"You're right."

"As much as I'd like us to focus solely on the safety of my daughter, we have to keep the whole picture in mind," John says, his eyes sagging. I want to kiss them until they smile. Can he be a father and still do this job? My heart is heavy in my chest because I don't know the answer to that question.

"We'll get some answers soon," I say. "I'm going to give Gina a call on my way home and update her on all of this." My voice is weak and dry and nothing like a professional. They both give me a tight nod and say their goodbyes, excusing my emotion. We could talk all night and not get anywhere. What we need is to get into Clare's life and get some actionable intelligence.

The night has become windy and I loosen my hair, letting it fly unconfined. The whip and tangle of the tree branches match the confusion in my head. When I shut the Tahoe door, the silence is so intense, I stop and close my eyes. I've felt stillness like this before, but when? I shuffle through memories until my eyes fly open, stunned by the answer—it was when I would pray, really pray. It's been so long since I've offered a sincere prayer and received an answer. Will God still listen to me after all the mistakes I've made? After what happened to Nahla? *There's only one way to find out,* says the voice in my head. I close my eyes and bow my head.

My words are clumsy and second-guessed, but voicing one fear makes it easier to voice another. Soon I'm pouring my heart out to a god I've desperately missed. When I end my prayer, I wait and listen and try to believe he'll answer me.

At first nothing happens. But then the air in my Tahoe changes. As the wind continues to rage outside, peace settles around me. And then I gasp. Words, bold and clear, fill my mind so completely there is no room for anything else, even doubt. I know what to do.

## 41

My heart beats steadily, my lungs take in air and calmly release it. I don't know how it will all work out, but I'm so sure of the answer to my prayer, I trust it. And I haven't trusted much lately, especially God. *He's always there for you,* says the voice in my head. I nod, though no one is here to see it.

I start the Tahoe and head toward the exit. After I pass security, I push the code on my ring for Gina, but I don't think she hears the click. The static of wind muffles her voice, but it's clear enough to hear her chewing out the unlucky tech guy who's with her.

"No, we can't go down. And don't you dare spill my Red Bull." I hear a frightened-sounding male voice respond but can't make out the words.

"Gina, are you still up in the bucket?" I ask.

"Yes, I'm still up here and I'm not coming down until I find some way into this woman's life." Maybe Gina *did* hear the click and just doesn't care. I wince with a mix of compassion for the tech guy and pride in Gina's effort.

"Tell me what you're trying to do," I ask.

"It's kind of a long shot, but I've got to try everything. Just a minute," she says. The wind lulls and I hear gulping swallows of what I assume is the Red Bull the tech guy is not supposed to spill along with the clicking of computer keys. "I only heard of this hacking method done a few times on the dark web." There's an awkward pause. "Okay, forget I said that last part. And what are *you* looking at?" I assume she asks the tech guy. More key clicking follows.

Her last gulp of Red Bull seems to have kicked in because she rattles computer jargon so fast, I can't keep up. Even if she slowed down, I wouldn't understand it.

"Gina," I say loudly to interrupt her. "Like I'm an idiot, okay?" She chuckles and apologizes.

"It's like finding a door in a dark hallway. The only way you're gonna find it is to actually be in the hallway which is why I'm up here in this box—I'm in Clare's cyber hallway. I can feel my way down until I come to the door. And it goes faster if there are two of us. Once we find the door, we can count the steps to find it again without having to be up here."

"So, once you find it, can you just open it and go in?" I feel dumb asking such a simple question for something so complex, but I need to understand.

"I'll have to write a program to get in, but my best guess it will take me maybe twelve to fifteen hours. If I can find the door before midnight, I can be in her world midday tomorrow."

"When you find the door, will she know it's us?"

"I think we'll have about twenty-four hours before she knows who's breeched her security. But that's just a guess. I'll know more when I actually get in."

"You're amazing, Gina." She snorts so loud it hurts my ear.

"I wanna know who's gonna pay for my detox program to get me off of Red Bull when this is all over."

"I will," is the muffled answer from the tech guy.

"Y'all just keep typing or we'll be up here all night," Gina snaps at him.

"Do me a favor?" I ask. "When you get in and find out what Clare's hiding, will you tell me first?" This request goes against everything I've taught my team. But the answer to my prayer was "get to Clare first" and this is the only way I know how to ensure that. Just the thought of not following through on that answer makes me sick. There's a long pause, so long I wonder if she heard me.

"Ya sure about that, boss?"

"Yeah, I'm sure."

"You doin' okay, honey?" Gina only calls someone honey if she's really worried. And she should be, because this request goes against protocol. I don't know why, but I have to reach Clare first and I can't let anyone get in my way.

"I'm fine. Just promise me, okay?"

"You got it." If my team is anything, they're loyal.

"And let me know when you find the door. You know, the whole door-dark-hallway thing is creepy, but it works." This makes her laugh, a sound I need to hear from her.

I thank her, tell her to lighten up on the tech guy and say goodbye as I pull into my driveway.

JAKE TURNED me into a fifty-something working woman in a charcoal maxi skirt and a black long-sleeved blouse. The

skirt brushes the ground when I walk, conveniently hiding a
good portion of my quick-change outfit. I'm wearing a wig of
mostly gray hair pulled into a bun at the nape of my neck.
My real hair is braided and wound into a large circle and
secured by a hair net. The pressure of it all pushes against
my scalp and I feel the beginning of a headache.

Clare is three cars up and over in a parking-lot-like freeway. She'll be late for work this morning. The man in the car
ahead of me is arguing with his wife about money. I have a
perfect visual of his mouth in his side mirror and can make
out every word he's saying. Apparently, he can't stay ahead of
his wife's online shopping and isn't too happy about the cost
of the recent kitchen remodel. I wish I were close enough to
read Clare's lips. She's been on her phone since the traffic
stopped.

I yawn twice in a row and reach for my cup of coffee. I've
been up since three when John called and told me Gina had
found the cyber door. She's at headquarters, tucked away
with her tech guys writing a program we hope will allow us
in the door and buy us some time before Clare knows it's us.

The coffee warms the back of my throat and I close my
eyes for a second, enjoying the sensation as it soothes the
pressure on my scalp. The few hours of sleep I got were deep
and dreamless. I haven't slept like that in years.

It was chilly this morning, and a few trees on my street
have leaves turning. Rose has trees in her garden that will be
spectacular in a few weeks. Livvy looked cute in her pink
jacket this morning, walking into daycare. I offer a silent
prayer that Eva can get photos of the drawings, and that
Denise will overhear some more information while driving
Livvy and her friends to preschool.

By the time we arrive at Harrod and Raynott, Clare is

forty-five minutes late to work. I almost lose sight of her as she flies down the sidewalk, her lavender stilettos clicking against the cement so quickly it becomes one continuous sound.

I spend the morning walking and watching, but there's no sign of Clare. I head off on another surveillance route when she comes out of the building. As usual, she's looking down at her phone as she walks, appearing lost in her own world. I try to always stay behind her, but because of the route I started, she's walking toward me.

I inhale through my nose and sink deep into my profile. My shoulders hunch a little, my hips stiffen and roll with each step. My gaze is on my phone and I force Clare's image to blur along with the rest of the people on the sidewalk. She's about twenty yards away when I hear a click in my ear.

"Kate, Gina's in the door. Clare knows there's a breech, but she doesn't know it's us," John says. Every part of me wants to react, but long years of training takes over. *Keep walking. Keep breathing normally. Keep my gaze in the same place.*

I'm ten yards away when Clare abruptly stops, looks up, and scans everyone around her. She knows.

omething on Clare's phone warned her of our
breech. She stands stock-still on the sidewalk as
people maneuver around her. Their only concern
appears to be not bumping into her. As soon as their path is
clear, they meld back into their oblivion. I have to do the
same.

I'm a few yards away from her. She's at a standstill, her
weight evenly distributed on both legs, her eyes narrowed as
she takes in everyone walking past. Her left hand still holds
her phone out in front of her. I allow my peripheral vision to
show my notice of her, like everyone else trying to avoid her.
I'm just feet away from her when John says, "Kate, if you
heard that, cough."

*I'm not Kate. I'm one of dozens of women on this sidewalk. I'm*
*tired and heading back to work, hoping the coffee I just drank will*
*get me through the rest of the day. My only concern about this*
*young woman in her ridiculous shoes stopped in the middle of the*
*sidewalk is that I don't run into her. As I pass her, as I feel her*

eyes sweep over me. As our shoulders align on the same plane and my lungs fill with her harsh scent, I cough. I'm sure this is a common social occurrence for her, wearing the perfume she does.

I begin a count in my head to gauge the number of seconds from where I passed Clare to the corner of the building—the gap. Once I turn the corner, I will execute my quick-change.

"Is she by you?" John asks. I cough again.

"Did she show signs of knowing?" Another cough from me. John swears under his breath.

"Quick-change. I'll count you down. Tell me when your gap starts." These are familiar words—quick-change, count down, gap. We've practiced it together so many times. The corner is almost here. Feet away. The count continues in my head.

I turn the corner. "Thirty-six," I say small and quietly. I have no way of knowing if Clare is still standing where she was, giving me at least thirty-six seconds until she could turn the corner and possibly see me. Adrenalin burns through me, as does the instinct to steal a glance back, but I can't. You can never look back. My gut tells me she's not behind me, though, and I have to trust it.

"Okay, here we go," John says. I exhale through my mouth. "One, two, three...." His voice is rhythmic and steady, just like in practice. I take a step with each number. My bag comes off my shoulder and in one fluid motion I turn it inside out, changing it from a plain black purse to a tan denim backpack. "Seven, eight, nine...." Hunching over as if I'm looking in my backpack with my face partially in the opening, I sweep my hand across the back of my head. I pull the bun on my wig, bringing it and the hair net into the backpack, at the same time draping my braid across my shoulder. "Fifteen, sixteen, seventeen...." In between strides, I give my maxi skirt a strong tug and in two more strides the deceptively lightweight fabric is a small ball in the backpack, leaving me in black yoga pants and Birkenstocks.

No one's head turns to look. Everyone seems focused on their phones. "Twenty-two, twenty-three, twenty-four...." Another tug and my blouse joins my skirt in the backpack. I'm wearing a tan tank-top with a brand-name logo on the front. "Thirty-one, thirty-two, thirty-three...." A tan baseball cap and aviator sunglasses come out of a zipper pouch in the backpack, and I'm a tourist in the country's capital. "Thirty-five, thirty-six." John completes the count and there's a pause as I zip up the backpack and sling it over my shoulder.

"Done," I whisper.

"Get out of there. Now." I dart across the street as an oncoming city bus pulls to a stop. I'm on it in seconds, choosing an aisle seat next to a teenage boy engrossed in something on his phone. He doesn't even notice me sitting down.

"Do you know where this bus stops next?" I ask the boy. He rolls his eyes and points to the electronic sign displaying in red letters the next stop. "Oh, Logan Circle. Thanks." It was a stupid question, but one a tourist would ask. It also allowed me to tell John I am safe, on a bus, heading away from Clare.

"Thanks, Kate. You did great. Let me know and I'll send someone to bring you in." John will also send someone around five this evening, dressed in my working woman disguise, to pick up my car. He'll cover every detail to keep me safe. This knowledge wraps around me like a warm blanket.

I smile a thank-you at the boy, but it's wasted. His attention is back on his screen. As the bus pulls away, I see Clare come around the corner.

## 43

I spent the afternoon roaming the National Mall and the surrounding area, taking photos of monuments and working my way through a few museums like a tourist. Two hours later, I'm on L'Enfant Plaza in front of the International Spy Museum. The sun had moved behind some clouds, casting strange shadows across the pleated glass front. I bought a black hoody and baseball cap to change my look. It was chilly, so it made sense—it was what the people around me were doing. And who would expect a spy to change her profile here?

When I was sure no one was following me, I contacted John, and he sent an officer to pick me up. As soon as I got in the car, I used the officer's phone to check in. Neal put me on speaker with John and my team as I relayed the tricky timing with Clare and my quick-change. The officer driving kept giving me side looks. When I finished and handed him his phone back, he told me I rocked and gave me a fist bump. My face warmed with gratitude. It was nice to be Kate again.

They're all waiting for me in the conference room. Neal's

the first to greet me, pulling me into a hug. "I'm so grateful you're safe, Katie." The relief of being in off the streets catches up with me and my contacts slide in the extra moisture filling my eyes.

Eva, Denise, and Gina all speak at once, giving praise and asking questions. There's a good deal of nonverbal communication happening, as well. John's eyes are busy, smothering me with kisses and some questions of his own. And Gina is demanding to know if I'm still serious about what I asked her last night. She won't let up until I finally give her a small nod. She grits her teeth and nods back. *You're doing the right thing* says the voice in my head. The assurance settles me and I give Gina a grateful smile. After a few more exchanges, she leaves to go back to her computer and tech guys who promise a program by midday tomorrow.

"Let's sit down and get you caught up," Neal says. I feel John's eyes on me and for the hundredth time I want to tell him everything—about praying and the answer and the connection I felt with God. But my gut tells me to keep it all to myself for now. For whatever reason, once we know Clare's plans, I need to get to her first. Seconds will matter.

I focus on the stack of files at the end of the table and sit down. John's eyes follow mine.

"These are copies of the drawings on Clare's refrigerator." John spreads eight-by-ten photos of various drawings in front of me. Some are of homes with people standing next to them. Others are a little harder to decipher. But what catches my eye are the dates—all written next to the word "playdate" and all future dates. Everyone remains silent as my attention bounces from one drawing to the next.

"Eva, are these the same drawings you saw before?" I ask.

"No. These are new. The drawings I saw all had dates in

the past." My eyes keep darting from one date to the next. One week out. Ten days out. Two days. There's no pattern or connection. I look up at Denise.

"Did the children talk about the playdate tomorrow?"

"Yes. They were asking each other if they had their drawings done. They seemed overly concerned about it. If the idea of bringing a drawing to the playdate came from the children, they would talk about it playfully. But they were serious and even stressed about it. This all has to be coming from the adults."

"Somehow Clare is working communication through these children. Could the other parents be a part of the cell?" I can tell by everyone's expression that they have spent the last few hours going over this very question and all the other questions it leads to.

"Everyone Clare has ever said 'hi' to checks out to be clean as a whistle," John says. "Gina can't find a thing."

"We have to get inside that playdate tomorrow," I say. "It starts at ten, right?" The Clare I saw on the sidewalk this afternoon was rattled, perhaps enough so to even change her ironclad schedule.

I look at Neal and he nods once and holds my eyes. I've worked long enough with him to know he's thinking what I'm thinking. "Something's going to happen at that playdate tomorrow," Neal says. He turns and looks at John and the blood drains from their faces. Is it from concern for Livvy or something more? *Just get to Clare first*, the voice in my head tells me.

～

THE MUSCLES in my legs ache as I climb the stairs to the attic room. I went running this morning and pushed myself harder than normal, trying to take the edge off the adrenalin I woke up with and that still courses through me. I feel sure of what I need to do once Gina's inside the cyber door, but beyond that is an unknown. And facing the unknown is frightening, no matter how many assurances you have.

I ran my usual path through the forest. It's good I had it memorized because the misty darkness only allowed me to see a few feet at a time. The mist has held on with the certainty of rain soon. It gives Clare's home an eerie dead look. There are no lights on, making it look even less inviting than usual, if that's possible.

Neal and Gina are back at headquarters, Gina and her tech guys still frantically working on a computer program and Neal coordinating teams of CIA officers and FBI agents to be ready for every probable scenario the playdate may reveal. John, Eva, and Denise will be here soon. We all want to be near during the playdate. For what, I don't know. The dozens of probable scenarios chased me through the dark forest at four this morning.

I'm dressed as a CIA officer today—dark pants and white blouse. But this morning I have my side arm in a shoulder holster hidden under a dark jacket. It's rare that an officer will feel the need, or ever use, their weapon despite what Hollywood says. Today is one of those rare times. I don't know what Clare has going on and I want to be armed. I say another silent prayer that Gina will find out soon and I'll be able to get to Clare . . . and know what to do after that. I adjust my earpiece to make sure it's secure.

Officers and agents move around me as the night staff briefs the day staff. The words "playdate" and "drawings" move from one worried face to another. Though he still has his gruff demeanor, I watch Agent Maxwell greet everyone he passes with a good morning.

I stay by the window and watch. The couple posing as the vacation renters come in from their morning walk, heads hidden by hoodies wet from the mist and hands tucked in their pockets against the cold. There are still no lights on in Clare's house.

"I thought I was early," John says behind me. I turn around and meet his searching eyes. I let them search and find my fear. "Any word from Gina?" he asks.

I pause for an extra second to consider if Gina said something to him about my request but immediately dismiss it. Gina wouldn't have done that. She understands that I need to know what she finds first, before John or anyone else. She trusts me. And I trust my answer. It may cost me to do what I need to do to get to Clare first. But my instincts tell me it will cost me and everyone else a great deal more if I don't.

"No word from Gina on my end," I answer.

"She'll get the program finished soon," and gives my arm a brief touch. I sway with the need to fold up against his chest, to have him hold me and tell me it will all be okay. I give him what I hope is an encouraging smile. I have to hold steady for a while more.

Denise and Eva show up, bringing John and me a cup of coffee from the kitchen. The smell of bacon and coffee had already made its way to the attic, and several people have gone down for a quick breakfast. My stomach rumbles at the smells, but I don't feel like eating. I take the coffee from Eva and smile. She looks like a worried mom, and so does Denise.

There's nothing to watch until parents drop kids off, but

my eyes keep moving to the window. We huddle around a small table and again go over all the information and photographs we have of the children and their parents. There are six—four girls and two boys. These parents are educated and well employed—lawyers, physicians, financial advisers. They drive nice cars, take nice trips, and associate with people like themselves. No red flags.

Time crawls. I check the clock on my phone as often as I look out the window. Voices and words circle in my head as my eyes move from one child's picture to the next. With each pair of innocent eyes looking back at me, Clare's presence—just a few hundred yards away through wood and drywall and glass—intensifies. With a straight shot, I could throw a rock at her. Through an open window, I may hear her. She's so close and masterminding evil I don't know, evil that somehow involves these unknowing children.

I clench my jaw and feel my earpiece move in my ear. It brings me a small sense of control. There's a pause in the conversation, and I realize it's been too long since I've said anything.

"Denise, tell me again what the children said yesterday, on the way back from Jarsdel," I ask. Her eyebrows come together in question, probably because she's repeated it many times. But she goes through it again carefully, phrase by phrase. I have it memorized, but I want to hear it again—the children's words. My chest tightens with the urge to be with these children, to see this unknown evil through their eyes.

I hear a car on the street and stand up so quickly I bump the table, forcing everyone to grab their coffee to keep it from spilling. My cup topples over, but it's empty. Denise rights it in one motion. It doesn't stop me, though, and I'm at the window in two strides. Ava has arrived. She's out of her booster seat and opening the car door before her mother can get to her. Her dark ponytail bounces along with her backpack as she trots to the front door. Her drawing must be in the backpack.

The coffee churns in my stomach as I glimpse Clare at the doorway. She moves to the side and Ava darts in the house. I take a deep breath through my nose and remind myself that hostage rescue is on standby, just a few minutes out.

A similar scenario plays out as the rest of the children show up. Sofia is next, followed by Emma and Charlotte, who come together with Emma's father. Alex is next, followed by Noah. Both are late and look as if they came straight from soccer practice. All the children come with backpacks and all appear to be excited.

People are talking around me, but I don't keep up. I offer minimal effort toward following—a nod or an "uh-huh." Clare shuts her door for the last time. All the children are with her, in her home. It's hard to take my eyes from the door to look at my phone. Another fifteen minutes have passed. And then another. It's almost eleven. Are they having lunch? Are they showing each other their drawings? Is Clare dating them with some system we haven't figure out?

Huge drops of rain hit the window and I blink. Rain comes heavier and heavier until Clare's house is a blur. John stands next to me, watching.

"Kate, waiting is the hardest part. But we have to find out what she's doing and who she's working with." I look at him and nod. I'm surprised by how well he can read my thoughts. But then again, I'm not bothering with masks right now.

The rain comes in waves, allowing me brief glimpses of

Clare's house. I rehearse in my mind, for the hundredth time, how I'd quickly and quietly get inside. The rain makes a great sound cover. I lost Nahla. I can't lose Livvy. I push these thoughts aside and search for the stillness that came with my answer.

John touches my arm and I flinch back to attention. His eyes cover my face with kisses. "I trust you," he says so softly I can barely hear him. I drink in these words along with his kisses. *Get to Clare first. It will all work out,* says the voice in my head. Before I can thank John, I hear a click in my ear.

## 44

"Kate." Gina's voice is frantic and breathy. "Clare's not using the children to communicate. The children *are* the weapon. She's training them to be sleeper cells. She's using videos, games, brainwashing. It's on her television right now. I'm counting to ten and then I'm telling the others."

There's a look we make when we realize we've been taken by surprise, when we've missed something, when we've been caught. They train spies to not only mask that look in ourselves, but also to recognize it in others. Just like Garza's men when they opened the SUV and saw the JIBs, I have that look all over my face. But I only allow John a glimpse before I turn and run.

I'm through the attic door and down the stairs, passing officers and agents with expressions that show me they're connecting the dots between surprise and recognition and reaction. I'm banking on the few seconds it takes to do this so I can get across the street.

I fly through the front door and am instantly drenched.

The pounding rain drowns out anything happening behind me, but I'm still able to hear John's voice in my ear.

"Wait, Kate. I'll come with you," he says. I can't wait. Not even for a second.

*Get to Clare*, says the voice in my head. So sure I am of these words, I yield my brain to them, allowing my instinct to take over and move before me. I'm over Clare's fence and make it to the side of her house in three strides. I step from the top of the garbage can to the block wall, then muscle-up onto the first-story ledge. The roof is slick from the rain and my hand slips into the drainage gutter. Pain slices through my palm but I don't stop to look at it.

"We're coming, Kate. We're right behind you," John says. I don't slow or look back. My brain clears a path before me and I instinctively move down it—a machine that has to get inside Clare's house.

I wrap the bottom of my jacket over my elbow and pop a hole in a window. I'm certain all kinds of alarms are warning Clare, and that's good. I want her to know I'm here, to come to me and move away from the children.

Carefully, I reach inside and flip the window lock. I hear movement on the ground below me but ignore it. A few more seconds and I'm inside what looks like a staged bedroom from a model home. I assume its Clare's bedroom —it reeks of her perfume and feels unlived in.

I step away from the window and broken glass on the white carpet. John is telling me he's coming, but I take my earpiece out and put it in my pocket. The quiet clears my head and I can hear the thrum of the television below and the thud of footsteps on the stairs.

Clare's coming.

I draw my gun and level it at the doorway. I'm sure Clare

has weapons hidden all over this house, but her hands are empty when she comes in. Her eyes meet mine and a slow smile moves across her face. "You're Miss Kate with the pretty eyes." Her voice is as high-pitched and annoying as usual, and she shows no recognition of the gun I have pointed at her chest. She's speaking to me, this monster I've been following for days. "I've seen you, on the street and in the Starbucks. Those old women were you," she says.

I focus on her actions, not her words. She has no weapons, but her hands are moving and twitching. My body shifts and prepares for a knife or blade to come at me. My instincts respond in kind to every movement of her body, preparing for her next three moves.

I hear commotion outside the window but remain focused on Clare. She fingers something in her right hand, and I shift and prepare. She lifts her hand to her mouth, almost reaching it when another hand—a tan hand I know —slaps Clare's away.

"Don't put that in your mouth," the person with the tan hand says. Eva. My focus expands and I recognize the red-and-white capsule that flew out of Clare's hand. It's lying inches from the wall, a dot of red on the white carpet. It was her weapon. She was going to kill herself with it.

My knees weaken with relief. Valuable intel would have died with Clare. But she's not dead. I was here, causing her to pause for a few seconds—the few seconds that kept her alive.

Another dark hand reaches up and lays warm fingers across my hand holding the gun. The touch travels up my arm in slow, steady rolls.

"Not like this," Denise says in my ear. My gun lowers

with her hand until it hangs at my side. She slips the weapon from my grip and I let her take it.

A man is standing behind Clare, putting handcuffs on her, talking quietly. He moves to the side and I recognize Agent Maxwell. We make eye contact as he finishes reciting the Miranda Rights. Clare is silent and stands erect. A jihadist in stilettos. She doesn't take her eyes off the pill on the floor.

Agent Maxwell's eyes move from me to Denise then to Eva. "It looks like you officers have done my job for me again." His rain-drenched shirt molds to his saggy chest and I can smell him over Clare's perfume. But his eyes are kind, thankful even. "Kate, go downstairs with the kids. We'll take care of this up here," he says.

Livvy. The children. My heart pounds to life as my feet take awkward, jolting strides through the doorway and down the stairs.

## 45

I stop two steps from the bottom when I see John come in the room. Gina must have been able to cut the video feed because the television screen shows a menu. Yet the children remain seated on the sofa, staring at it with their backs to me. As soon as they see John, though, they fly to him like magnets. Their high-pitched words are a jumble, with Livvy the loudest.

"Dad, can I go with you?"

"I want to go home."

"I don't want to be here."

They crowd around him, little hands gripping his shirt and pant legs. Their desperate fear makes the back of my throat ache. It's not just Livvy who sees John as a father, but all these children—a father, a guardian, a protector. John did what he had to do to make sure the evil that threatens these young lives will never harm them, even if that evil is his ex-wife and the mother of his child. There really *are* fathers like this and John's one of them. Neal was right. Not all divorced men are like my father

John softly assures the children, touching each one on their shoulder or head. He sees me and the children's attention follows. Livvy runs to me and wraps her arms and legs around me so I'm forced to sit down on the step. I curl around her embrace, her warmth reminding me how wet I am. She seems to not notice. "Stay with me," she says, over and over.

John came to his daughter first. Does he know what happened upstairs? *He'll know soon enough and it will all work out,* says the voice in my head. I bury my face in Livvy's hair and close my eyes. These children are safe. That's all that matters.

IT'S ALMOST midnight when I walk out of headquarters. The past twelve hours have been a blur of debriefing and paperwork. I drew my weapon on a supposedly unarmed suspect, acted outside the knowledge of my partner and team, and took Gina along with me—these were just a few of the actions I had to explain. But I was calm and ready to explain everything when I met Neal and my team. For the first time in months, I had trusted my instincts and because of it, Clare was alive. I had done the right thing, but will I still have a job? And what about John? And us?

Neal and my team had every right to be angry with me, but they weren't. They made sure I had dry clothes and hot coffee. An older female officer with a soothing voice bandaged my cut palm. Then they let me tell them why I did what I did.

I sat straight, faced them squarely and told them about praying and the answer I received. When I finished, three beats of silence passed. Their expressions were a search for words. Gina found hers first.

"Well, note to self. Less Red Bull. More prayin'."

The laughter was a balm to my soul.

"I'm proud of you," said Neal, the father of my choosing.

"You did the right thing," said Eva, the woman most like my mother.

"I would have done the same thing," said Denise, who with one glance can read my mind. Gina, voiceless and crying, pulled me into a hug and smeared my "ugly" white agency blouse with mascara.

"It's late and we could all use some rest. But John would like you to stop by his home tonight, no matter the time," Neal said to me. "We'll have some matters to deal with here, but don't worry, Katie, it will all work out." *It will all work out.* The same words the voice in my head told me at Clare's. I keep rolling these words through my head as I drive to John's.

There's a light on in the front room. I had to surrender my phone to the CIA, so I have no way to let John know I'm here. But he must have heard me drive up because the door opens as I come up the walk.

By the time I'm in his arms, I'm sobbing. Feeling him hold me and tell me over and over that I did the right thing is the best feeling I've ever had.

He leads me into the kitchen and gives me a wet washcloth. I hold it against my throbbing eyes and breathe in the cold fabric-softener scent. I hear him getting me a glass of ice water. When I pull the washcloth away, he hands me the glass. At the first taste, I feel parched and down the glass and another. The throbbing in my head eases and I close my eyes for a second at the relief.

When I open them, I see John for the first time since I got here. He's in a navy T-shirt and jeans. His eyes are sagging, red, and pop out of his pale face. But he's smiling at me.

"Let me see your hand," he says, gently taking my left hand. Aching fills my chest as I watch him examine the bandage.

"John, I'm so sorry." Of all the things I want to explain, these are the only words that will come out of my mouth. I watch the tears fill his eyes and spill down his cheeks. It's hard to see someone cry for the first time, to come apart in front of you. I wrap my arms around him and pull him to me. I want to hold him together.

"I need to talk to you," he whispers in my ear. His chest jerks as he chokes on the words. I nod and we walk out into the lighted garden. The only place not lit is Rose's cottage, and I offer a quick prayer that she's curled up next to Livvy right now. The fountain is on and we sit on the bench next to it where we can talk freely.

"How's Livvy?" I ask, not waiting for him to start. He wipes his eyes and smiles.

"She's happy to be back here. All she knows is her mom had to leave quickly on a work trip. But she kept asking me why she had to watch such a scary movie." His voice cracks on the last word and he pauses a minute to breathe. I'm gripping his hand so hard it must hurt, but I can't let go. "I can't stop thinking about what Clare was going to do to my baby girl."

I hold him as he sobs and there's a part of me that wishes Eva hadn't slapped that cyanide pill out of Clare's hand.

"How is Rose?" I ask after a few minutes. He wipes his face on his shoulder and laughs.

"She thinks you're a hero. She said she would have done the same thing." There's one more person who thinks this.

"John, I have to tell you why I did what I did. Why I asked Gina to tell me first and why I didn't wait for you." He turns a little so he can see my eyes. I tell him about praying and the answer I received. "For the first time in months, I felt sure of myself. I didn't know why I needed to get to Clare first until I saw the cyanide pill in her hand."

"When I told you I trusted you, I meant it. I'm glad you told me this, though." His eyes bathe my face with kisses as he tucks a strand of hair behind my ear. "When I found out what Clare was, I thought I'd never trust myself, my judgment, again." I wince with understanding. "But I wouldn't be much good to anybody like that. I had a daughter to take care of and a job to do."

"How did you get past it? The self-doubt?"

"I prayed. And the answer I got was to forgive myself and move on." I stare at him for three long seconds. How did he do that? Can I forgive myself for Nahla? "The more I forgave myself, the easier it was to trust myself and others." I want to curl in on myself, but I don't.

"I need to forgive myself for some things." It's all I can share right now. But it's a step. He wraps his arms around me and I melt into his chest. I could stay here forever.

"Well, today you did the right things. And it saved a lot of lives." I pull back and look at him. Livvy and her playdate friends were safe, that I know. But I wasn't given any information about the results. As far as the CIA is concerned, the minute I left Clare's house, I was off the case—no one is to discuss it with me, not even my team. So, I know John's not supposed to tell me what he's about to tell me.

"Clare knew it was us the minute Gina accessed her

video feed. If you wouldn't have been in her bedroom and stalled her for those few seconds, she would have taken the pill and we would have never found the other cells."

"You found who she was working with?"

"We did. When Gina accessed Clare's video feed, she could also deactivate her phone, which she did right before she told you. Clare had no way of contacting the other cell members, so I'm sure they trained her to take herself out and let the rest of the cell carry on the mission. The FBI picked them up an hour ago." Relief waves through me. I fold over and put my face in my hands.

"All the children are safe?" I ask through my fingers.

"All the children are safe. It was a success." He pulls me up and takes my face in his hands. "There'll be an investigation and you may be at a desk for a while, but it will all work out." I cover his hands with mine, pressing the warmth of his skin against my cheeks.

"I'm good with that."

## 46

J
ohn was right. I've been at a desk for weeks, doing mounds of mind-dulling paper work. But John's office is just down the hall. And two doors down from that is an empty office no one ever goes in . . . except us.

I see my team a lot, especially Gina who is completing several new computer programs for the Agency while driving her tech guys crazy. We've all been a part of an investigation, but Neal assures us that U-Tap will have many more operations ahead of us.

Harrod and Raynott Financial is undergoing a big, ugly investigation. They claim they were not aware of Clare's terrorist activities and have a horde of legal minds trying to prove it. Yet, clients are jumping ship daily. The same thing is happening at Nithercott Daycare and Jarsdel Preschool, forcing parents to brawl over open spots in daycares and preschools they would have never considered a few months ago.

As Neil suspected, Clare had started rumors about John

hoping to prove him an unfit parent and demand sole custody. When that wasn't working, Clare moved to Plan B—asking to have Livvy for a long period to make up for her summer of traveling. This uninterrupted time would give Clare the chance to begin Livvy's and the other children's "training."

Agent Maxwell and Eva tag-teamed until they got information from Clare. Eva's teaching Agent Maxwell some of her interrogation tricks and says he's coming along nicely. Clare was working with two other women, one parent like Clare and the other a female employee of Jarsdel's. Each was doing what Clare was doing—using playdates to turn children into terrorists to be activated years later. All together we saved fifteen children.

Denise has been working with the counselors for the children and their parents, and the outcome looks hopeful. The "training" Clare and the other women had begun had not reached what the counselors refer to as an undoable level. The future dates on the children's drawings were the dates believed by Clare to be when each child was ready for such life-altering training. Their goal was to create cells of children who on the outside appear normal but on the inside are the ultimate weapon for jihad—at some point in that child's life they would hear a certain phrase which would turn them into killing machines with no conscience.

What *will* be life altering is that three families have moms that are going away forever. How will the children ever come to understand and accept that? Livvy thinks her mom is on another business trip and is happy to be back with John and Rose, in a neighborhood with toys and bikes and sidewalk chalk.

But the day will come when Livvy will need to know the

truth. Knowing the truth will be better for her in the long run. The worst truth is less damaging than what your imagination can conjure up to fill in the unknown. This is one of the many things I've learned at my weekly counseling sessions Neal is not letting me get out of. And yet I'm not ready to fill in the blank of who my father is. Someday I will be. When I am, I know I won't face it alone. I'll have John with me.

I push the thought of my father away and realize it's the first time I've pushed thoughts from my mind in weeks. *You can have a hall pass for this one,* says the voice in my head. I smile and focus on the task in front of me. It's Thanksgiving Day and John and Livvy will be here in an hour to pick me up. They invited me to enjoy the feast Rose has been preparing for days. I'm also invited to attend church with them on Sunday, which I plan on doing. If I'm going to forgive myself, I'm going to need some help.

I stop and breathe in the scent of cinnamon and nutmeg. The apple fritters I just made—a surprise for John—are cooling on the kitchen counter. But I must focus and finish what I'm doing.

The box is half full and I still have two more walls to clear. I pull each pin from the wall and put them in a dish. I stack each paper in the box, careful to keep them in order. I'll come back to this, to who gave Nahla up, to who caused her death. But for now, all this information will be in a box in my attic.

I wind the string into small balls and stack them in the box's corner. My eyes move over the people I've hunted for months, trying to keep their faces from taking hold of my mind. I have told no one about this, not even John. I will someday. But for now, it will be in this box, waiting for me.

And my crazy room will just be a room with a bed and a nightstand and a lamp. Maybe Eva can stay will me next time she comes. Livvy could take a nap in here when she and John are over. I remember seeing Paw Patrol bedding online.

My hands keep moving and packing as I let my mind wander the normal things I could use this room for. Before I know it, the box is full and my walls are empty. I move in a full circle, taking in the clear, empty white of the walls.

I tape the box shut and pick it up. It's heavier than I expect. For a second, I consider just putting it in my closet. I am wearing a new dress, red with cream trim. And I'm sure my attic is dusty. *You need to have it farther away*, says the voice in my head. She's right. It's awkward and bulky, but I finally maneuver it through the opening in the ceiling of my hallway. As I climb down the ladder, I hear a knock at the door.

Thank you for reading *The Perfect Spy* all the way to the end! There's more to come with Kate, John, and the team. Sign up for my Newsletter here to find out when *Hold Your Breath: An Untapped Source Book Two* comes out.

If you enjoyed *The Perfect Spy*, will you leave a review? You will have my undying appreciation.

"But I never know where to do this?" May be your next thought. I'm with you! Amazon doesn't exactly make this easy.

*But I'm going to try.* Click on this link and you'll be exactly where you need to be. And if you're reading this in a paperback, you'll have to type this link into a web browser and at the same time earn even more of my undying appreciation. **Thank you!**

http://www.amazon.com/review/create-review?&
asin=B08S7L7T23

# IN THE MOOD FOR A SMALL TOWN ROMANTIC COMEDY?

*The Secret Obituary Writer: A Clean Small Town Romantic Comedy* is a laugh-out-loud, heart-warming romance that feels good to very last page! Click here to order.

*"The most entertaining book I've read in ages."*
*"Hilarious!"*
*"So much fun to read!"*

# THE STORY CONTINUES . . .

*The Secret Obituary Writer: Book Two* is a fun read full of plot-twists, with a HEA you don't want to miss! Click here to order.

*"Just as good as the first one!"*
*"Lively, hilarious, and full of suspense."*
*"When I finished the book, I was smiling."*

## ALSO BY AMY MARTINSEN

Changing Worlds

Marriage Hints for LDS Newlyweds

Hints for Latter-day Saints' Golden Years

# ABOUT THE AUTHOR

Amy loves to read.

One of her earliest memories is hiding between bales of hay to read *just one more chapter* instead of doing her chores. When her mother discovered this hiding place, Amy learned to climb trees and became very good at balancing on a branch while holding a book. She also developed extremely strong leg muscles. Now Amy still hides to read, but in much less dangerous places, like her closet and the laundry room...though she longs for the leg muscles of her youth. She also makes it her goal to write stories so engaging people will hide to read them. Perhaps even in a tree.

Visit www.goawayimreading.com to sign up for Amy's newsletter and find out what she's writing next.

Made in the USA
Las Vegas, NV
29 May 2021

23887901R00142